PARANORMAL COZY MYSTERY

Sparks & Landmarks

TRIXIE SILVERTALE

Sittin' On A Goldmine Productions, L.L.C.

info@sittinonagoldmine.co

www.sittinonagoldmine.co

Publisher's note: This is a work of fiction. Names, characters, places and incidents are products of the author's imagination or are used fictitiously and are not to be construed as real. Any resemblance to actual events, locales, organizations, or persons, living or dead, is entirely coincidental.

ISBN: 978-1-7340221-2-4

Trixie Silvertale
Sparks and Landmarks: Paranormal Cozy Mystery : a novel / by Trixie Silvertale — 1st ed.

[1. Paranormal Cozy Mystery — Fiction. 2. Cozy Mystery — Fiction. 3. Amateur Sleuths — Fiction. 4. Female Sleuth — Fiction. 5. Wit and Humor — Fiction.] 1. Title.

CHAPTER 1

It's a big day in Pin Cherry Harbor and, despite the great lake that now lies frozen to the shore of our fine city and the brisk February winds swirling up the snow in a way that reminds me of the dust devils that would rise up without warning back in the Arizona desert, there are several hundred people crowded along the sidewalks on both sides of Main Street.

The boulevard is completely blocked off between Second and Third Avenue, and the Pin Cherry Historical Society has constructed a temporary stage in the middle of Main Street, smack dab in front of my favorite eating establishment.

The mayor is decked out in his official garb, which for some reason includes an enormous top hat, and a sash bearing his title, embellished with hand-painted pin cherries. He mounts the steps to the platform, and thunderous applause ripples up and down the street.

"Good citizens of Pin Cherry Harbor, today is an historic occasion!" His breath hangs in the frigid air like a miniature word cloud.

Eager for any excuse to move at this temperature, tumultuous applause accompanies a smattering of chuckles—for his wordplay regarding the Historical Society, I assume.

"Our very own Myrtle's Diner is celebrating its fortieth anniversary."

More cheering, followed by two officious looking women and one scowling man climbing the stairs toward the mayor. "Ladies and gentlemen, let me present your Historical Society board."

Far less applause and several murmurs.

I raise an eyebrow and look up and down the rows of gathered townspeople. Even without using my extrasensory powers, I would have to say the Pin Cherry Historical Society is not a beloved organization.

The wise, and apparently eternally disappointed, male member of the trio approaches the microphone. "Good citizens, it is with great pride that the Historical Society presents this award to Mr. Odell Johnson. His effort to meticulously protect the historical authenticity of his establishment for lo these past forty years is admirable indeed."

Cheers of "Johnson! Johnson! Johnson!" echo through the street, and I applaud as loudly as my wool-mitten-clad hands will allow. Far be it from me to mention that his "meticulous efforts" are a direct result of his penny-pinchery rather than any sort of affection for history.

"Mr. Johnson, please join us."

Shielding my eyes against the impotent, late-afternoon sunlight, I search the crowd, but don't see anyone moving toward the stage. However, I do recognize the flame-red bun bobbing atop my favorite waitress's head. Tally, despite her age, weaves through the crowd like a teenager.

Her diner-raised voice resounds over the noise of the crowd. "He's still flipping burgers! Give me a minute." She disappears into the diner named after my dearly departed grandmother, who was a founding partner. Odell was not only her first husband, but also my first friend in Pin Cherry.

Tally returns a moment later dragging a belligerent Odell behind her. She's forced him to remove his apron, but I'm very pleased to see he hasn't put on any airs for the occasion.

She tugs him onto the platform and I see a glimmer of the old Army cook beneath his exterior as he stands at the position of attention waiting for the committee to dismiss him.

One of the female members of the trio approaches the microphone and adds her approximately two and a half cents to the occasion. "I would be remiss if I didn't mention Isadora Duncan, also known as Myrtle Johnson back in the day. I'm sure you all remember our spitfire local celebrity. She was both an ardent supporter of the Historical Society and possibly our largest violator."

There's a smattering of snickers and several cheers.

I may not have lived here that long, but it seems to me you either love or hate the Historical Society. Somehow Grams managed to walk the razor's edge, but it sounds like her biggest posthumous supporters are part of the *opposition* party.

"In honor of the diner's fortieth anniversary, the Historical Society and the Chamber of Commerce will be sponsoring an open house at Myrtle's Diner this evening, and next week our very first, hopefully annual, Valentine's Day Taste of the Town will be hosted by all the businesses along Main!"

The third and final member of the trio approaches the microphone. "Tickets for 'Taste of the Town' will be available at Myrtle's Diner and the Piggly Wiggly until the thirteenth. Now, it is my honor to present this award for historical preservation to Mr. Odell Johnson."

More clapping and a few shouts about "best burgers in town."

Local newspaper photographer, Quince Knudsen, who works for both his father's paper the *Pin Cherry Harbor Post* and his school's newspaper, threads his way through the crowd, snapping pictures with his 35mm camera. Believe me, I was as shocked as you are to meet a high-school student who embraces the old-fashioned art of film photography.

But I should mention that Pin Cherry, in general, seems to be the town that tech forgot.

The award is a statue of Lady Justice holding her scales, which I find an odd image for a Historical Society trophy.

"Mr. Johnson, please accept the Historical Society's highest award, the 'Scales of Balance' premier historical honor, for your fine efforts in providing delicious food to our community for decades while preserving the historical importance of your establishment."

Odell steps forward, runs a hand over his utilitarian grey buzz-cut, and accepts an awkward handshake. Of course, he doesn't hold it nearly long enough for the photo op.

If only I'd known, I could've given him quick "mugging for the camera" lessons.

"Now, before we all head into the diner to have a celebratory meal, would you like to say a few words, Odell?"

A faint smile touches his mouth and the wrinkles around his coffee-brown eyes deepen as he steps up to the microphone and with his classic—call it charm—offers the following commemorative phrase, "If you folks expect me to serve two hundred burgers today, I best get back behind the grill instead of standing up here waggin' my chin."

Uproars of laughter fill the street as Odell leaves the stage with the speed of a pursued gazelle and hightails it back into the diner.

The mayor grabs the microphone to make a few closing remarks, which I don't hear because the rush of humanity pushing for the diner sweeps me along like a flash flood in a dry riverbed.

I manage to dive to the side just before I'm swept into Myrtle's, and I struggle upstream on the sidewalk to get back to the bookshop and bring Grams up to speed on the big happenings.

Slipping the antique brass key from around my neck, I admire the heft of it in my hand. Back in Arizona, when I received a strange manila envelope containing this key, a wad of cash, and my grandmother's last will and testament, I was months behind on my rent and dangerously close to being fired from my barista job.

Never in a million years did I imagine that this key would open a bookstore—and so much more. It unlocked a whole new world of family, belonging, and psychic powers. I slide the triangle shaped barrel into the lock and twist three times. I can sense Grams on the other side.

As soon as I open the heavy, intricately carved wooden door, her ghostly eyes light up with excitement. She adjusts her strands of pearls and smooths her silk-and-tulle Marchesa burial gown. "Did they mention me? Did they say anything about me at the ceremony?"

I inhale the welcome, bookish aroma of home and chuckle. It's hard to believe that this woman who died before her time, in her sixties, is the same phantom standing before me at her chosen ghost-age of thirty-something. But despite her lack of a physical body, clearly, her ego is still intact.

"Mizithra Achelois Moon! I'll have you know, this has nothing to do with ego. I'm simply proud of what Odell and I created together."

I point meaningfully to my lips. "Grams you know the rules. If these aren't moving, you're not allowed to respond. No thought-dropping. Don't we have a deal?"

She shrugs and vanishes through the wall.

"Don't be like that. I'll tell you all about it."

Her head pops back through and her eyebrows arch eagerly.

"The lady from the Historical Society said something about you being their biggest supporter and their worst violator."

The remainder of Grams' ghostly form bursts through the wall and her ring-ensconced fingers land in a fist on either hip. "Violator? She called me a violator? The nerve of that—" Her golden-brown eyes spark with indignation.

"Easy, Isadora! I'm not sure if that was the exact word."

"Well, I don't care what word it was. I donated more money to that society than they ever earned!"

"Is that how you got away with your lavish renovations to this historical building?"

Grams opens her eyes in affected offense. "I'm not sure I receive your meaning."

"Honestly, Grams, you pretty much gutted this place. I mean, secret doors, massive closets, museums, garages . . . I don't think any of it's historically accurate."

"Well, I protected the brewery's building next door and put several measures in place to keep the historical authenticity of those stables and employee sleeping quarters intact. The Historical Society simply showed their appreciation for my efforts by extending some leniency toward me on my proposed renovations for the bookshop."

"I think that's called a bribe."

The front door opens and Grams vanishes like smoke in the wind. I turn to offer my assistance to the potential customer, but my greeting shifts to a huge grin when I see the welcome shadow of my father outlined against the six-by-six windows.

"Dad!"

My grandmother's only son, Jacob Duncan, strides toward me. He towers head and shoulders over me, but that head is topped with the same absolutely white-blonde hair as mine and we also share our mysterious grey eyes. His broad shoulders stoop and he scoops me into a warm hug. "How's my favorite, *and only*, daughter?"

I laugh at his addition to the greeting. After far too many surprises about family members I never knew existed, my father knows better than to insinuate he might have another daughter out there somewhere. I may have lost my mother far too soon, but transforming from an eleven-year-old orphan, hopelessly lost in the foster system, into a twenty-one-year-old heiress with an amazing father and a generous Ghost-ma, goes a long way to making up for lost time.

"We set up in back?" My father's question

seems to be rhetorical, and I smile warmly as he makes himself at home.

I don't need the Historical Society to tell me how special Pin Cherry Harbor is—my heart confirms that every morning when I wake up, with the loving ghost of my grandmother fussing over my every whim in the swanky apartment I inherited.

If my friends could see me now! No, seriously. After I opened the door of my rundown studio apartment in Sedona, Arizona, and discovered an inheritance—my life changed drastically. I ran out on several months of back rent (which I've since repaid) and a dead-end barista job (no reparations there). I jumped on a bus filled with other refugees from the human condition and landed here, in Pin Cherry Harbor.

It wasn't an easy adjustment, and I've made my share of mistakes. In fact, if you were to ask the handsome local sheriff, I've made nothing but mistakes. But let's get back to my original point: it's Friday night and normally I'd be out on the town making bad decisions, but, instead, I'm sitting in the back room of a magnificent three-story bookshop, that I now own, and I'm playing Scrabble. My cohorts are my only employee, who works for the entertainment, not the money, my long-lost father, and Ghost-ma.

And I'm definitely starting to think Grams cheats at Scrabble.

"Now you listen here, young lady. I have never cheated on anything a day in my life!"

I repeat the claim for the other players' benefit, since I'm the only living person who can hear my grandmother. We all share a hearty chuckle at Grams' expense.

"Myrtle Isadora Johnson Linder Duncan Willamet Rogers, I'd have to say that any woman with that many husbands and this much money"—I gesture to the enormous bookshop, which is home to a staggering amount of first editions and rare occult tomes—"must've cheated on something at some point."

"Well, I never." Grams crosses her bejeweled limbs over her ample bosom and juts her chin out haughtily in my direction.

"Methinks thou doth protest too much, Grams."

Twiggy smirks as she places her word on a triple-letter score. "H-U-S-S-Y."

As Grams watches Twiggy add the tiles of insult to injury, her ethereal eyes widen and she vanishes through the nearest wall to escape our mockery.

"Grams, Grams," I call after. "I seem to remember you telling me that you won Pyewacket in an 'off the books' Scrabble game."

"Reow." Pye rotates his black-tufted ears like tiny satellite dishes and licks one large tan paw.

In case you don't speak caracal, that definitely sounded like "can confirm" from our resident spoiled-rotten fur baby.

Grams pokes her head back through the wall to defend herself. "I hardly think it was cheating. I simply did what was necessary to save this poor creature from a horrible exotic animal dealer who was starving him nearly to death."

I smirk as I muse, if ghosts had halos . . .

"Mizithra! I think—"

"Grams, how many times do I have to tell you? No thought-reading." I point meaningfully to my lips. "Just because you can, doesn't mean you should."

Grams swirls back to her place at the table and adds, in my general direction, "Sounds like good words to live by."

Now it's my turn to be shocked. "Excuse me? What exactly are you implying?"

Even though Twiggy can't hear my grandmother's side of the conversation, she's pretty quick on the uptake.

Her chopped grey pixie-cut remains immobile as her brown eyes cut back and forth between the empty fourth chair and me. "Are you two having one of those 'pot versus the kettle' discussions?"

My father chuckles softy.

Both my grandmother and I ignore Jacob and stare at Twiggy with manufactured surprise.

Twiggy cackles mercilessly.

And this would be the compensatory "entertainment" I mentioned earlier.

She catches her breath and continues, "The way you chase poor Sheriff— What do you call him? Oh right, Sheriff-Too-Hot-To-Handle! The way you chase him around this town, it's as if he's a slab of raw meat and you're a half-starved dog."

My dad blushes uncomfortably as he looks from Twiggy to me.

Grams joins in the laughter and seems relieved to have the spotlight removed from her questionable past.

I choose to take the high road and ignore the not-entirely-slanderous remark. "Regardless of what you had to do to get him, I'm happy to have Pye and this bookshop."

My extrasensory skills may still be under development, but it doesn't take an advanced-level clairsentient to feel the wave of guilt rolling off Twiggy. "Are you cheating?"

Twiggy goes still as a corpse and avoids making eye contact. "You don't know what you're talking about, doll."

Grams looks at me and her spectral eyes twinkle. "I think you're onto something, Mitzy."

I run a hand through my wild haystack of white-blonde hair and chuckle. "So, takes one to know one, huh?"

Twiggy leans back in the stiff wooden chair and puts her hands up like it's an old West train robbery. "All right, you got me. I mighta pulled one or two extra letters along the way."

Grams slams her ghostly fist on the Scrabble board and actually manages to create enough solidity in her energetic limb to upset the tiles.

My father jumps reflexively, and his eyes dart left and right. "Mom?"

I pat Jacob's hand reassuringly. "Yes, it was Grams having a snit."

Twiggy scrapes back her chair and marches away from the table. "That's enough Scrabble with spoiled heiresses and moody ghosts. I gotta get home and feed my dogs."

"Reeeee-ow." Pyewacket hisses a warning and his stumpy tail flicks with irritation.

"Don't worry, Pye. She would never bring them here."

Twiggy leans down and scratches Pyewacket's arched back. "They wouldn't last two minutes with this overindulged wildcat."

Pyewacket purrs loudly and seems to nod his head in agreement.

As Twiggy, in her ever-present biker boots, stomps toward the side door into the alley she stops in the glow of the red "Exit" sign and turns back toward me.

"Did you forget something?"

She shakes her head.

I glance down at my enchanted mood ring and I see a bingo card. "Does it have something to do with bingo?"

Her shoulders jump with surprise and she nods slowly.

"You're getting so good at interpreting the messages, dear." Grams attempts to pat me on the back. However, without the weight of strong emotion behind it, it feels about as solid as pulling a spider web off a sweater.

"What is it, Twiggy? What do you need?"

She shrugs and picks at one of her fingernails, but doesn't reply.

My father is an astute observer of body language. He stands abruptly and says his goodbye. "I should get going too. I'm heading out for some ice fishing for a couple days, but we'll have breakfast at the diner when I get back."

"Copy that." I smile and give my dad a big hug.

He slips past Twiggy and disappears into the

frosty darkness. A cold blast of frost-scented air chills the room in his wake.

Now that my dad has left, Twiggy appears unusually self-conscious. She looks down and taps the toe of one boot. "I was wondering if you'd come to bingo with me tomorrow night?"

Oh brother, first I'm playing Scrabble and drinking "pop" on a Friday night, and now I'll have to spend my Saturday at a bingo hall! Am I twenty-one or eighty-one?

Grams sends me a quick telepathic message. *You know Twiggy never asks for favors. It might be important.*

I nod and proceed with caution. "You didn't set me up on another date did you?"

Twiggy cackles loudly. "Not even close. I think Artie's cheating at bingo, and you're the next best thing to a lie detector in these parts."

After a lingering eye roll I agree. "I'll come to the bingo hall with you on one condition."

"Name it, doll."

"You get me into one of these 'off the books' Scrabble games."

Twiggy shakes her head. "Your funeral." She clomps out the side door and it slams shut loudly as Grams chuckles behind me. "Funerals aren't as bad as she thinks."

CHAPTER 2

SATURDAY MORNING DAWNS at the bright and early (by my standards) hour of 10:00 a.m. After a rousing game of "try to catch the fiendish feline," I wind up clinging to the highest rung of a narrow wooden ladder, which stretches from the second-floor balcony to nearly the top shelf of two stories of bookshelves. When Grams converted this old brewery into the Bell, Book, & Candle Bookshop, she kept the utilitarian mezzanine that curved around the massive brewing vats, but replaced all the piping with custom oak shelving.

From my precarious perch, I stretch as far as I can and my fingers dance across the tomes on the highest shelf of my bookshop, releasing puffs of faery dust. Honestly, it's good old mundane dust, but in a place like this I feel the need to class up my jargon.

"Glad to see you're finally taking an interest in your inventory, doll." The anything-but-dulcet tones of my volunteer employee, Twiggy, pierce the cavernous quiet. "I'm not sure what kind of a get-up that is, but it doesn't seem real conducive to reachin' the high places." A satisfied guffaw punctuates the air as her boots clomp out a retreat down the metal leaves of the spiral staircase.

It's probably best that she left before I can explain my reindeer onesie pajamas or the reason for my early morning ladder acrobatics.

Between you and me, the PJs are a nostalgic reminder of my meager, pre-inheritance existence in the high desert—before I relocated to almost-Canada. However, the catalyst of my climb is none other than the furry demon spawn: Pyewacket.

Oddly, when Grams left me this place, she neglected to mention that I would also receive a fiendish feline who would steal my good underwear and hide it in the uppermost recesses of the aforementioned bookstore's shelves.

And you heard me right. "Good underwear." I'm an heiress now, with a philanthropic foundation and everything, so I have fancy panties—and plenty of them. Regardless of the fact that I could simply purchase more every time Pye raids my drawer, I take personal offense to wasting money.

Reusing coffee grounds until the filter ripped and taking cold showers in a dodgy studio apartment are not yet distant memories. Every once in a while, I might forget how lucky I am, but—

"What in Aunt Sally's casserole are you doin' up there, dear?"

And now I have another reason to find some fresh underclothes. "Grams! How many times have I told you to use the slow, sparkly reentry when you return from whatever ghost realm you disappear into?"

Bejeweled limbs cross impatiently, and ring-ensconced fingers absently play with one of her pearl necklaces. "I don't actually go anywhere, dear. You know I can't ever leave this bookshop. I just go into a low-power mode and you can't see me, I guess."

"You guess?"

"Well, I haven't been in the ghost business all that long. It's not like there was a manual or something, like in that one movie with the girl and the parents."

"*Beetlejuice*? Are you making a *Beetlejuice* reference right now?"

Grams waves her ghost arms as though she's

trying to hail Charon. "Don't say it a third time! That's how you activate him!"

Her eyes are wild and I can't stop myself. "So, you actually think that if I say *Bee—*"

A surprisingly firm ethereal hand clamps over my mouth with undeniable corporeal force. The shock and the strange tactile sensation of energy that has no weight, but somehow has strength, subdue my voice.

But I happen to know her little secret. So I simply think as loud as possible, *Beetlejuice!*

She, of course, hears my thoughts.

We both wait with bated breath, which is obviously more of a big deal for one of us.

No freaky, striped uber ghost appears from the beyond.

"You're making real progress with affecting objects in the material world with your poltergeist-powers. But never believe what you see in the movies, Grams. I may be a film school dropout, but even I know that no matter how many times you say a ghost's name, they rarely do what you tell them." I raise an eyebrow in her general direction.

"Oh, Mitzy! You're such a card." Grams hugs me and smooths my hair back from my face so she can plant a ghost-kiss on my forehead.

The emotion of the moment takes over, and I forget that I'm still several rungs up a ladder.

My foot slips.

My arms flail.

My bottom-heavy backside gives gravity its due.

You know that scene in the movies when everything slows down and the person's life flashes before their eyes or they dodge bullets—that does not happen.

I rocket toward the earth, which is all the way down on the first floor. The u-shaped ends of the former brewmeister's walkway are quite narrow and barely have room for the twenty-foot ladder, so, as I slip backward, I'm heading over the railing on what seems like a one-way trip.

So, when something rams me in the back and knocks me away from the hand-carved banister and onto the thin strip of balcony, I naturally go catatonic.

"What in the blazes is all the commotion?" Twiggy stomps out of the back room, waits a beat, and clambers up the circular staircase.

The woman who served as my grandmother's closest friend in life rushes toward my sprawled body with more concern than I would've imagined possible. In general, she doesn't much care for my twenty-something shenanigans. "Mitzy?" She bends down and looks intently into my grey eyes. "Did you hit your head?"

Grams is whirling like a dervish and alternating

between panic over my crash landing and glee over her new ability.

My brain is unable to process either.

Twiggy shivers violently. "Isadora? That you? What the heck happened to the kid?"

Since Twiggy can neither see nor hear Grams, she doesn't receive an answer.

And before either of them can choose a course of action, Pyewacket saunters over, bites the elastic band of the underwear that is somehow still in my hand, and takes off on a mad tear.

That does the trick. "Robin Pyewacket Goodfellow!" I lift my head and watch him disappear into the stacks.

"Looks like you'll live. You better stay off the ladders until we can get you a safety harness, Your Highness." Twiggy shakes her head and chuckles all the way down the stairs. "There's ice in the freezer," she calls as she descends.

I rub the back of my head and take several deep breaths. "Grams?"

"Right here, dear. Are you all right? Did I hurt you?"

"Hurt me? I think you probably saved my life! I mean, I'm not sure if a thirty-foot fall would kill me, but I'm pretty sure it would've come close." I caress the golf-ball-sized lump on the back of my head as I gaze up at the narrow ladder stretching toward the tin-plated ceiling. "How did you do that?"

Grams is grinning and rubbing her hands together. "I'm not sure, you know. I've been working on my writing, with the pen and ink in the museum area, but I've never picked up anything heavier than a book—until today."

"Careful." I narrow my gaze and shake my head.

"Oh, Mitzy, you always know how to make me laugh." Grams giggles. "I wasn't making any judgment about anyone's weight. I'm just amazed that I could lift a human. It was only for a second, and I was so terrified you'd be injured . . . maybe that's what gave me the power."

"Should I call Silas?" My grandmother's former lawyer, who is now my lawyer, also happens to be a vastly skilled alchemist and the person responsible for tetheringGrams to this bookstore. I'm still learning exactly what an alchemist is, but I've personally seen him heal wounds, influence others, and put some kind of spell on an old pair of glasses that allows him to see my Ghost-ma. He's been searching through my collection of occult books for a way to hear her, but, in the meantime, I get plenty of work as an afterlife interpreter when the two of them need to chat.

I'll have to deal with my four-legged thief later.

Right now, I desperately need breakfast and, more importantly, coffee.

A quick change into a sweater and a coat warm enough to withstand the February chill, and I'm off to Myrtle's Diner.

I hustle through the crisp air and push my way into the welcome warmth inside the diner.

Odell looks up from the grill and salutes me with his spatula through the red-Formica-trimmed orders-up window.

I wave back, inhale the familiar smell of comfort food, and slip into an open booth.

A steaming mug of coffee slides across the silver-flecked white table. "Mornin', Mitzy. You have any Valentine's Day plans?" Tally pokes a pencil in the flame-red bun that sits tightly atop her head, and her crows-feet crinkle as she smiles.

I reflect on my current dating life as I ponder my answer. Having been on a few dates with an enigmatic local antiquities dealer, I assume he'll make some plan. But my efforts to attract the attention of our handsome local sheriff have been fruitless. However, I don't think Tally needs to hear the sad details of my uneventful love life, so I simply reply, "We'll see."

Odell walks out and sets a plate of lovely scrambled eggs and chorizo with a side of delectable home fries in front of me.

"Maybe I'll just plan on more of this." I bask in the aroma and grab my fork.

"But you probably wouldn't turn down an invite from Sheriff Harper, if one happened to fall into your lap." Odell raps his knuckles twice on the table and walks back into the kitchen as his shoulders shake with laughter.

Did I mention how everyone knows your business in a small town? Well, they do. Regardless, I'm finding comfort in routine. When the center of my universe, my mother, was taken from me, I lost my way. I drifted aimlessly through the foster system and picked up far more in the way of bad habits than good. Having a touchstone like Myrtle's Diner, with its friendly atmosphere and predictability, soothes my wandering soul. Maybe I watched too many episodes of *Cheers*, but sometimes it's nice to go "where everybody knows your name."

Odell taps his spatula to get my attention and calls from the kitchen. "Any big plans for your Saturday night?"

I laugh much harder than I should. "Apparently, I'm accompanying Twiggy to bingo."

His eyes widen in surprise.

Tally rushes over and fishes some tip money out of her pocket. "Will you play a card for me? I usually go, but Tilly is forcing me to help her decorate for the Ladies Luncheon Club Valentine's Day Lonely Hearts Luncheon.

I swallow my initial response regarding whether or not it will be held at the Department of Redundancy Department and instead ask, "Does she host that every year?"

Tally clutches her chest in shock. "Hardly! This is her first year. It's a huge honor, for sure. That's why she's going overboard. It's not that I mind helping her, you know. But bingo is so much fun. It'll be a real shame to miss it."

Talk about taking a sip from a fire hose. I think that's the most Tally has ever said to me. "Sounds wonderful. I'd be happy to play a card for you." I refrain from telling her that I've never "played a card," and I have absolutely no idea what I'm doing. I go with my gut and add, "Here's to a bingo!"

Tally grins widely. "Maybe two!"

I lift my mug in a gesture of celebration, gulp down the rest of my coffee, and skedaddle out of there before I volunteer for any additional nonsense.

The Elks Lodge bingo hall is nothing like the ones I've seen in the movies. And as a film aficionado, the letdown is rather heartbreaking. I expected thick clouds of smoke to hang from the ceiling, while feeble geriatrics hunched over stacks of bingo cards and flicked their ashes into overflowing ashtrays.

This place, though it's seen its share of decades, is clean and well lit, and smells of cleaning supplies. The hall is host to a broad age range of men and women engaged in lively banter.

Twiggy grabs us a seat next to Artie, the local snowplow operator, who vigorously pumps my arm in greeting as her grey-brown curls bounce in unison.

"Mitzy Moon, as I live and breathe. How are you doing? How's that cantankerous Odell? You know he still owes me money from that bet he lost in 1983."

I chuckle as I try to match the enthusiasm of her handshake. "Well, you know Odell still makes the best pin cherry pie in town and I eat far more than my share of meals at his diner!"

Before she releases my hand, she leans in close and unsuccessfully attempts to whisper, "How goes your pursuit of local law enforcement?"

My face turns red as a radish and I drop her hand. But before I can defend myself, Twiggy jumps in to my NOT rescue.

"She's still throwin' herself at him like pasta at a wall, but nothin' seems to stick."

The two tough old broads enjoy a lengthy

chuckle at my expense before the caller mounts the platform at the front of the hall and calls for order.

Twiggy slides three bingo cards and a dauber my way and explains the basic concepts. The rules of bingo aren't difficult, but it's also not as easy as you might assume. Especially when you have to keep track of multiple cards.

Some random person is chosen from the audience to inspect the bingo balls and equipment. Once he or she finds the gear satisfactory, a "thumbs up" is flashed to the players in the hall.

After the "rando" returns to his or her seat, the game begins.

"This first one's a Four Corners call. Best of luck to all in the hall!" The caller grabs the handle on the bingo cage and turns it two full revolutions before tipping the cup, sending a ball down the shoot, and calling out, "B-17." Then he drops it in some kind of holding cup and cranks the barrel two more times.

I may be the first twenty-one-year-old to actually die of boredom.

Twiggy leans over and whispers in my ear, "Picking up anything?"

Right. I completely forgot I was here to investigate the alleged cheating. I glance down at my grandmother's magically enhanced mood ring, but it's not offering up any answers. To be clear, it definitely takes its name seriously and only supplies helpful clairvoyant messages when it's in the "mood."

I shake my head, and Twiggy gives me a stern look indicating I better step up my game.

The caller up on stage continues to crank the barrel, call the numbers, and place the balls in the holding cup.

As I watch events unfold, I honestly can't imagine how one would cheat at this game. Calls are random, cards are preprinted, and everyone hears the same number. I've only placed two stamps total on all three of my cards, two of which are for Tally, and I'm sure the caller has pulled about eight or ten balls from the container. Somewhere at the front of the room a hand shoots up and the call "Bingo!" echoes through the hall.

A smattering of clapping mingled with groans and possibly boos follows.

The winner brings her card up and the caller checks it. She fiddles with her bright red curls and tugs at the edge of her fuzzy pink sweater while the caller examines her card. Once the verification is complete, she's given some slip of paper, which I'm assuming is a "hey you won this round" receipt.

"Get ready for a no doubt blowout. The next one is a Texas Blackout!" The caller cranks the handle and smiles.

Twiggy leans over. "Anything?"

I shake my head. The only thing I'm sensing from Artie is that she's hungry. I scan the room to see if any refreshments are provided, but all I see is a poorly stocked vending machine in the back of the room. I lean toward Artie and ask, "Can I get you something from the vending machine?"

Her eyes light up like a Mississippi gambling boat and she replies, "I wouldn't say no to a bag of sour cream and onion potato chips."

I pat her on the back as I get up from the table and walk toward the vending machine. I select a bag of sour cream and onion potato chips and a small pack of chocolate chip cookies.

Heading back to the table, I pause to survey what has become my life. From this angle, at the side of the stage and the playing area, I notice something I didn't pick up on initially. The pink-sweatered winner is sitting at the very front table, facing the stage, and she seems to be very animated for someone playing bingo. I cross my arms and watch her more closely.

Hold on just an apple-picking minute! The caller sure is paying a lot of attention to Pink Sweater and the calls are coming fast and furious. I close my eyes for a second and bring her face to mind. She isn't unusually attractive and she isn't even wearing a low-cut blouse. I realize that's fairly stereotypical, but most stereotypes exist for a reason. And men do tend to glance at cleavage when it's displayed. No judgment. Just stating the obvious.

Making my way back to my table, I leave the pack of cookies for Twiggy and hand the chips to Artie. I lean down and whisper, "I need to stretch my legs. Will you watch my cards, Twiggy?"

"Already doing it, Your Highness."

I shrug and make my way over to the opposite side of the bingo hall to get a better look at our winner. By the time I reach the far wall, I see Artie's hands go up. "Bingo!" she calls.

The caller looks more shocked than I would've expected. I mean, it *is* bingo night at the Elks Lodge after all, and people calling out 'bingo' seems like it shouldn't be a surprise.

Artie gets her card checked and receives her slip of paper.

Pink Sweater makes an odd face at the caller. A new game is announced and eight or ten calls later Pink Sweater's hand goes up again. "Bingo!"

The caller checks her card and she receives another slip of paper. This win is met with far less applause and far more booing. Seems Pink Sweater won the money ball "double-jackpot" round.

Glancing down at my spelled mood ring, I see a blank bingo card. Not a huge surprise. Looks similar to the bingo card image I saw when Twiggy invited me. But when the hairs stand up on the back of my neck I'm forced to pay closer attention. Why a blank bingo card? After three wins why does my ring show me a card with no squares stamped? I think it's time for Mitzy Moon to get on the case.

I make a trip to the water cooler at the back of the room and fill a cup far too full. Of course, in the movies when people carry beverages the cups are generally completely empty, which has always annoyed me. You see, it's very easy to tell if someone is lifting an empty mug or gesticulating wildly with an empty cup of coffee. Just because you put a lid on a coffee cup doesn't mean you can wave it around like a baton. If there were any coffee in that cup it would spill. Rant over.

Heading up to the front of the room, I attempt to squeeze between the first table and the platform. Now, I'm no string bean, but there's plenty of room even for these hips. So a bit of acting is going to be required to pull this off. I wiggle and twist and trip and spill my water all over Pink Sweater and her bingo cards. She gasps and knocks her chair backward as she stands and attempts to wipe the water off her sweater and very wet jeans.

While she's distracted I take a quick mental picture of her bingo cards. They are blank. All of her little stamps have been placed along the border at the top. Not one single square is stamped. I find that odd. Don't you? How exactly do you win bingo without marking off a bingo? No need to make any further scene, but you can be sure Twiggy's gonna hear about this.

Hustling back to my table, I'm rudely interrupted before I can make my report.

"Miss, you'll need to come with us."

Twiggy chuckles. "Don't give 'em any trouble, doll. I'll catch a ride with Artie."

So much for my acting skills. The bingo hall goons escort me out and give a warning regarding "shenanigans" and "horseplay" and about how troublemakers get added to their blacklist.

Oh, you best believe I'm on that list!

CHAPTER 3

I'M PLEASED to report that I have a rich inner fantasy life and try to make a point of dreaming frequently about gorgeous, upstanding, slightly Dudley-Do-Right-y Sheriff Erick Harper. In this particularly imaginative episode, I'm enjoying a romantic, utopian Valentine's Day dinner with said sheriff, when—

"Mitzy! Mitzy! Wake up! Fire!"

I sit bolt upright and rub my eyes furiously. If you've never had the displeasure of being awakened from a lovely dream in the middle of the night by a ghost, let me get you up to speed. It's terrifying! Any one of those things, by itself, would be shocking, but all of them together—horrifying! I throw off the covers and leap out of bed.

"Where? Do we have a fire extinguisher?"

"The fire's next door, sweetie. Look!"

I gaze out the large six-by-six windows on the side of my second-floor apartment, and the night sky is ablaze with orange. The brick building next door is fully engulfed in flames and the odor of the black smoke has already seeped into my room. I may be wearing a magically enhanced mood ring, but I don't need extra-sensory information to know that brick buildings don't burn that hot or that fast, in February, without an accelerant. I whip off my reindeer onesie and start layering up for warmth.

Silk long johns. Wool socks. Lined snow pants. Extra-thick, down puffy jacket. Stocking hat. Thick, wool-lined leather mittens.

As I run to grab my phone from the nightstand, a loud explosion cracks the night air.

I may have screamed. "What was that?"

Grams shrugs her ghost shoulders. "Could be the old furnace next door?"

"Where's Pyewacket?"

"He ran out of here through whatever secret passage he uses as soon as I sounded the alarm. I've never seen a fire spread so fast, Mitzy."

"I know, Grams, it's not good."

"You'd better call Silas. He'll know what to do."

I slip off one mitten and call my alchemist-attorney as I race to find Pyewacket.

"Silas you better get over here! What? No—

There isn't time for manners! The building next door to the bookshop is on fire— I don't know how big. Like really on fire!"

The call abruptly ends and I have no option but to assume he'll comply.

"He's on his way, Grams." I hit the plaster medallion above the intercom and activate the secret bookcase door. Before the wall has time to fully slide open, I squeeze myself out and run across the second-floor Rare Books Loft as I call for Pyewacket.

No reply.

I thunder down the circular staircase and, of course, trip and fall over the chained "No Admittance" sign. Oh, if I survive this night, Twiggy is going to get a piece of my mind.

"Pye? Pye, where are you?" I hear the tiniest whimper and crawl across the floor toward the children's book section. There, tucked between a first edition of *Alice in Wonderland* and a tiny turnip plushy, is my caracal. His black-tufted ears lie flat against his head and his fangs are bared, even though he looks more frightened than frightening.

"Come on, Pye. We gotta get outta here, sweetie. We gotta get out of here, right now."

I'm worried if I grab him, he'll scratch the living daylights out of me, but there's no way I'm leaving him inside. I move toward him and reach slowly toward his middle.

After a hard thwack against my mitten, I discover the thick leather is actually quite protective. So I scoop him up, claws and all, and run to the front door. Holding a struggling wildcat with one hand and undoing custom tumblers with the other is no easy task. Somehow, I manage to unlock the door, and as I push it open Pyewacket rockets out of my arms, tearing a giant hole in my down jacket with his hind claws. But I couldn't care less. He's out. He's safe. I hope he doesn't freeze to death escaping the fire. There's irony in there somewhere, but I have no time—

"Miss Moon. I was just coming to check on you. Everyone out of the bookshop?"

Erick looks very official in a thick winter uniform coat and his deerstalker hat. If my stomach wasn't churning so hard with terror, it might feel just a tiny bit tingly at the sight of his tall, muscular frame. After all, I call him Sheriff-Too-Hot-To-Handle for a reason!

"Yeah, we're out. It's just me, and Pye jumped out of my arms . . . so there's no—" *Great Gatsby*! I can't tell him that I've left a ghost behind. What am I going to do? Grams is inside. Completely trapped. She can't leave the bookstore. If I can't get her out of there, and this thing catches fire . . . Oh geez, I don't know what to do. Silas. I need—

"Mitzy, are you all right?" Erick places a hand on my shoulder and leans toward me with concern.

"I need Silas."

"I'm here, Mitzy. I've just arrived."

Erick waves to Silas. "All right, Mitzy, you stay with Silas. Odell's opening the diner, so you'll have somewhere warm to wait this out. We'll do everything we can to save the bookshop, but this fire is extremely volatile. You two head down to the diner and stay safe." And with that, Erick rushes back toward the sea of red and blue lights swirling around the fire trucks and squad cars.

I can't move. I'm just staring at the flashing lights and the roaring flames, and I can't move.

Silas puts a hand on my shoulder and whispers commandingly in my ear, "Come with me." He leads me away from the emergency vehicles on First Avenue, around the corner of the bookshop and down Main Street, to where it dead ends above the gorgeous, iced-over great lake nestled in Pin Cherry Harbor.

"Erick said to go to the diner."

"Erick doesn't realize how much we have to lose."

I come hurtling back to my senses. "Yes! That's

why I needed you. Grams is trapped in there. I can't lose her, Silas. I can't *actually* lose her."

"I will perform all the transmutations in my power to make sure that doesn't happen."

When we reach the back of the bookshop, Silas darts behind my three-story brick building with surprising agility for a man his age. I notice his usual scuffed leather shoes have been replaced with heavy winter boots, and he trudges through the snow so quickly I can barely keep up.

"I got Pyewacket out. He jumped out of my arms and I just—"

"That infernal feline has at least seven good lives left. Don't you worry about him." Silas waves away my concern as easily as if I'd mentioned the snow in February. "I may need your help with this."

"With what?" When I reach the corner of the bookshop adjacent to the alley, which is the only thing separating my beautiful bookshop from the towering inferno next door, Silas motions for me to stop.

"Are you wearing the enchanted mood ring?"

I nod.

"Please remove both your mittens and grasp my left hand with your two."

I don't know what he's got up his sleeve, but this is the man who taught me how to get out of handcuffs with only the power of my mind, so I'm not arguing.

"I need you to focus on the snow and ice surrounding us. Clear your head and heart of all other concerns. Fill your mind solely with snow and ice. As if this great body of water, which is now frozen, is sliding across the beach, up the embankment, and swirling through you."

Closing my eyes, I do my best to ignore the raging blaze next door as I imagine the ice taking on a life of its own and somehow flowing through me.

Silas places his right hand directly on the brick wall and I hear him mumbling something ancient under his breath. It sounds a little like "galoshes free goose," but I'm sure it's more complicated and Latin-y than that.

I close my eyes again and force myself to focus on the ice, but I just keep thinking of Grams and what will happen if the bookshop catches fire.

Silas twists his left hand and grips both of my wrists. "You must focus, Mitzy. Your grandmother is counting on you."

My mind instantly goes blank and the only thing I can see, hear, or feel is the ice. I can visualize it now, in my mind, sliding through me like a slow-moving glacier across Greenland. I feel energy pulsing up from the snow, drifting through my body, and into Silas's hand.

"That's it, Mitzy. That's perfect."

Time evaporates and I am only a vessel for this icy flow. Eventually, the weak, grey light of dawn breaks through the thick cloud cover and I open my eyes.

The building next door is a charred, angry carcass. The scent of ruin coats my lungs. Blackened spires of broken brick jet toward the sky, and thick white smoke lies like a blanket over the ruins. But the flames, the flames have died.

My bookshop stands, completely unscorched by the conflagration.

But before I can thank the man who saved Grams from the void—

He collapses into the snow. "Silas!" I slap his thick jowls and hold my ear close to his face. I can barely feel his breath against my cheek. I've got to get help.

I run full speed down the alley and hit a patch of ice, where overspray from the firemen's hoses has frozen to a sheen, and slide headlong into Deputy Paulsen.

She goes down with a thud, but flips onto her belly and pulls her gun so fast I feel as though I might still be dreaming.

"Stand down, Paulsen. Stand down. It's only Miss Moon." Erick walks over, reaches down a hand, and pulls me to my feet. "What exactly are you doing out here, Miss Moon?"

"Silas . . . He's collapsed."

"Paulsen, get an ambulance over here."

"10-4, Sheriff." Paulsen reluctantly holsters her gun and presses the button on her radio to summon the paramedics.

Erick leaves me slipping and sliding on the fresh patch of ice while he hustles down the alleyway toward the limp shape in the snow. I eventually find my balance and carefully shuffle across the slick surface, but when I reach the far side of the impromptu ice rink, a chill of a different kind shoots down my spine.

I turn toward the charred building and gasp. Someone was inside. I don't know how I know. I think that one is claircognizance. Whichever one it is, one of my psychic senses is screaming at me and the world around seems to slip away.

Gaining some traction on the ash-covered snow, I run toward Erick and Silas. As I arrive via the alley, the paramedics and a stretcher are running in behind the bookshop from Main Street.

They scoop Silas from the drift and strap him on the gurney, rushing away before I can tell them anything.

Erick rubs his eyes and his shoulders sag. "Take good care of him," he calls after the medics.

I awkwardly pat Erick on the shoulder. "Thank you."

He turns and places one hand on each of my shoulders. As he leans down, his piercing blue eyes knife into my soul. His stare reveals the pain he must have suffered, losing good men during his Army tours in Afghanistan.

My heart breaks a little and I clamp my mouth shut.

"I told you and Silas to go to the diner. What were you doing dragging that old man out into the cold in the middle of the night? He's probably got smoke inhalation, frostbite, maybe a heart attack . . ."

I have to tread lightly. I can't reveal what I've seen in his eyes, and I can hardly tell Erick that it was Silas who dragged me out in the cold, in the middle of the night to perform some transmutation of fire into ice to protect my bookshop and my grandmother's ghost from permanent erasure from this planet. So I'll try a different tack. "There's a body in that building." I gesture to the smoking remains. "Do you think it could be Rory?" Erick and the owner of Bombay Antiquities and Artifacts aren't friendly, but I hardly think Erick would be happy to hear that Rory died a horrible fiery death.

"Why would it be Mr. Bombay?"

"When I first came to Pin Cherry that building

was vacant, and the last person I remember poking around there with a realtor was Rory. It was around Christmastime. If there's a body in there, it could be his." My voice cracks and I shudder involuntarily.

Erick takes off his hat and runs a shaky hand through his lovely blond hair. It's usually perfectly slicked back and very professional, but clearly he was awakened in the middle of the night and this messy, tousled look is incredibly distracting.

"Did you see someone go into the building last night, Miss Moon?"

"No."

"Did you see lights on in the building last night?"

"Well, no." I chew the inside of my cheek.

"Then why on earth would you assume there's a body in the building?"

He's got me there. I can't exactly say that I received a psychic message. I've already indicated that I didn't see anyone go in or see lights on inside the building, so I'm running out of options. Looks like I'm going to have to lie my way out of this one. "I heard some noises last night."

Erick squints suspiciously, but pulls out his notepad. "About what time did you hear these noises?"

"After midnight." Since I didn't hear anything

before I went to bed, and I probably fell asleep about midnight, if I'm fabricating a story this seems like a good one.

"How would you describe the sound?"

What kind of question is that? He clearly doesn't believe me and he's simply trying to trip me up with his early morning interrogation. "I don't know, Erick. Noises like— Noises that shouldn't be in an empty building."

Erick shakes his head in frustration and saunters down the alley as he speaks into his radio. I watch him walk away, as usual, but decide to follow close enough to hear what he's saying.

"Check the county records and let me know who owns this building. We need to notify them it's a total loss. And while you're at it, see if you can get confirmation on whether or not the building was vacant."

Well, at least he believes me enough to follow up.

"Re-ow."

Erick spins around. "Moon! I told you that thing has to be on a leash."

"Pye! You're alive!" I crouch down and hug my fiendish feline until he nips my ear. "Don't be like that, Pye. I know that you said 'thank you' a second ago."

Erick chuckles. "Get him inside or get him on a leash, Moon."

"All right, I'll take him inside and give him his breakfast. Then how about you meet me at Myrtle's and I buy you a 'thank you' breakfast for saving my bookshop, before I head over to the hospital?"

The frustration and exhaustion melts from his face and is replaced by a grateful smile. "That'd be real nice, Moon. I'll meet you there in ten."

I nod casually and hightail it back into my bookshop through the side door from the alley. Once inside, I jump up and down like a fool and stifle an excited scream. After everything I've tried to get this man to go on a date with me, I never imagined a 'thank you' breakfast would be the ticket. I rush into the back room and plow directly into the solid wall that is Twiggy.

"Easy, Tiger, I thought it was your Grams who played roller derby! With a hip-check like that you could be blocker, no problem." Her cackle fills the room, and I can't help but laugh along.

"What are you doing here?"

Twiggy shakes her head. "Oh, you expect to set the building next door on fire and threaten my livelihood, and you think I won't show up?"

"Your livelihood? You don't let me pay you. You work for free."

"It's a job isn't it? Woman's gotta keep busy."

She pours herself some coffee and walks out of the back room, stopping at the door long enough to say, "Funny, I thought Silas would be here."

Hot tears spring to my eyes and I have to stop pouring Pyewacket's Fruity Puffs because I can no longer see the bowl.

"What's the matter, doll?"

"Silas was here. He saved the bookshop."

Grams rockets through the wall and I drop the box of sugared cereal. Fruity Puffs scatter hither and yon.

Twiggy shivers. "Is that Isadora, or are you just clumsier than usual?"

"Grams— Silas is—"

"What happened, dear?" Her kind ghostly eyes flicker with emotion.

"He was doing something to protect the building and then he collapsed. I don't know what to do."

Grams swirls around me in a panic. "You better get to the hospital and make sure he's all right."

"But I was just about to have breakfast with Erick."

Twiggy rolls her eyes and exhales loudly as she walks out.

Grams takes the direct approach. "Your dating life can wait, young lady. You get your little behind down to the hospital tout de suite, and you make sure my dearest friend is going to be all right!"

I shove a handful of Fruity Puffs in my mouth as I walk to the door. I'm not happy about being bossed around, but it does bring a smile to my face when I realize she said my "little behind."

CHAPTER 4

If practice makes perfect, then I should be approaching near faultlessness. I've made more trips to the Birch County Regional Medical Facility during my short time in Pin Cherry Harbor than all of my previous hospital visits put together. In fact, I might even recognize the nurse at the front desk. As I approach to get Silas's room number, I remember who's waiting for me at the diner. "Excuse me, I'll be right back." I nod and smile at the nurse as I dart toward the nearest potted-plant-filled alcove.

Fishing my phone out of the pocket of my coat, I immediately call the sheriff's station and ask them to patch me through to my breakfast date. Don't worry, I actually used a professional tone and said Sheriff Harper and everything. "Hey, Erick, I'm so sorry. I must've been in shock this morning. No—

No, I didn't forget. I'm at the hospital. My— I mean, I just thought I should check on Silas. Can we reschedule our date for lunch? Sure. Um, all right. Understood."

Let me give you the short version of Erick's side of that conversation: It's fine. He doesn't have time for lunch. It wasn't a date.

I obtain the necessary information regarding the room number for Silas, but when the nurse says he's in the sixth floor psych ward, even I know that's cause for concern. I step off the elevator and hastily make my way to room 607.

I stop abruptly in the doorway. The man fighting against his restraints in that hospital bed bears no resemblance to the calm, elderly, sedate Silas Willoughby.

Rushing into the room, I gasp at his normally milky-blue eyes, which are now a deep shade of charcoal. Not to mention the rivulets of sweat streaming down his temples.

"Silas? Silas what's wrong? How can I help you?"

"I'm sorry, Miss, he won't be able to respond. We had to give him a high dosage of sedatives. When the paramedics brought him in, he was raving wildly about how cold he was. He kept saying he was freezing. But you can clearly see he's overheated. Upon arrival, his temperature was

101.3, and it continues to climb. If the medication doesn't take effect soon, we'll be forced to take more drastic measures."

I need to be alone with him, to communicate with him somehow. Maybe psychically or something else, but first I have to get rid of this doctor.

I shake my head in disbelief. "Understood. I'll sit here with him and call the nurse if there's any change in his condition."

The doctor finally exits, and I sit back to survey the man in the hospital bed. I glance down at my mood ring, but the cloudy black swirls whirling inside the cabochon offer no clue as to how I can help. There has to be something I can do. This morning he asked me to grasp his left hand and push the cold into him. Maybe if I can reverse the process somehow, I can reverse the effects of whatever he did to quench the blaze.

I take his right hand in mine, close my eyes, and try to visualize pulling the heat out of his body. Within moments I feel searing heat in my hands. I breathe deeply and try to pull more. The flames are licking up my arms and my focus wavers. I force myself to concentrate, but the heat overwhelms me and I collapse backward into my chair.

When I open my eyes, Silas Willoughby is resting comfortably on two freshly fluffed pillows. His skin has returned to its normal pale, liver-spotted hue and the perspiration previously drenching his face is gone.

It would probably be best if I slip out quietly and let him continue to sleep. I lean forward to get out of the chair and my legs collapse beneath me. The chair slides violently across the linoleum and crashes into the pulse-ox monitor, setting off some kind of alarm.

A nurse hurries into the room. "Miss, are you all right? Did you faint?"

I push myself up on all fours and open my mouth to respond.

"She'll be fine, ma'am. She is blessed with a natural lack of coordination."

The nurse shakes her head and leaves us.

I turn just in time to see Silas enjoying a chuckle at my expense.

"Silas! You're all right!"

"It appears your visit was most auspicious."

"You saved Grams!" Tears well up in my eyes as I struggle to haul myself back up and pull the chair next to the bed.

"May I enquire as to how you managed to assist me?"

"I have no idea, Silas. I don't even know what was wrong with you. I just— The doctor said when they brought you in you kept saying you were so cold, but when I looked at you, it seemed like you were burning up. I thought maybe it had something to do with all the energy stuff from this morning, so I tried to reverse the process."

"A practical approach. And you were successful?" He steeples his fingers and bounces his soft chin on the tips of his index fingers.

"I'm not sure if I would call it a success. Whatever I did pulled some of the heat from you, into me, and then I must have I passed out."

"The art of transmutation is a delicate balance, Mizithra. I truly am in your debt."

I grip the rail on the side of his bed and lean toward him. "What are you saying right now? If I hadn't come to the hospital— If I hadn't known what to do— Are you saying that saving the bookshop could've killed you?"

He casually smooths his grey mustache with his thumb and forefinger. "We will all pass beyond the veil one day. While I do not imply that I will welcome that transference, I know this: my life on this side of the veil has been enriched by knowing you."

Hot tears spring to my eyes and, in spite of his "harrumph," I throw my arms around him and hug him tightly. "Thank you." Releasing him, I stand next to his bed. "I don't know what I'd do without you either, Silas. Now, I better get back to the bookshop and let Grams know that you're all right, and then I need to figure out some amazingly unforgettable way to apologize to Erick for standing him up at breakfast."

Silas nods. "I have always found pastry to be a delicious and heartfelt apology."

I flash my eyebrows. "Hmmm. I've got just the thing!"

My winter driving skills have improved considerably during my first season of true snowfall in almost-Canada, and as I park my Jeep beside the bookstore, I can't stop from enjoying a miniature seated happy dance. Who would've thought that this aimless orphan would one day reunite with the father she never knew and live with the ghost of the world's most wonderful grandmother? Certainly not me!

As I wandered from one unfulfilling barista job to another, crisscrossing the state of Arizona from Tombstone to Sedona, I had given up on happily-ever-afters. But now, every day I wake up to a town that is genuinely coming to feel like my home, and I get to hang out with my amazing grandmother. Plus, I'm finally getting to know my father. As a child, I dreamed he would come back to my mother and me. I've since learned that my mom never wanted a relationship with my dad; they just had a fling. But she wanted me—and until a commuter train struck her car and stole her away from me, the two of us were really happy together.

I assure you that over six years in the foster care system was not a path I would've chosen, but ultimately it brought me to my father and gave me the chance to build a relationship with him on my own terms.

Another squad car passes through the barricade on First Avenue and brings back images of my sleepless night and narrow escape. Personal reflection time is over. I need to update Grams, Twiggy, and Pyewacket. And after that, I better hustle on down to Bless Choux, the patisserie on Third Avenue, and find a way to both apologize and bribe Erick. Because you and I both know, I'm going to get to the bottom of why there was a body in that building.

CHAPTER 5

"Twiggy? Grams? Pyewacket?" Where is everyone? I hurry up the iron spiral staircase, pull down the secret "candle handle" next to my copy of *Saducismus Triumphatus,* and watch the bookcase slide open to reveal my hidden apartment. "Grams? Grams, where are you?"

At some point during my months of orientation to this labyrinth of a bookshop and printing museum, I recall Twiggy mentioning how much my grandmother loved the third floor museum displays. I'm on it.

I hustle across the mezzanine, down the stairs, and through the "Employees Only" door that leads from the front of the bookshop into the printing museum.

I have to admit that I love the atmosphere of the

museum. My mother read to me every night, and I've always loved the smell of books, so I relish basking in the bookshop's scents. However, the smell of printing presses is like the essence of books condensed down to their base molecule. It's comforting, and it reminds me I need to start a new book.

Snaking through various printing presses on the first floor, including an original Gutenberg press, I hurry up the two flights of stairs to the third floor.

"Here comes the thunder," calls Twiggy.

Grams sails across the room like a kite in the wind. "How is he? Did you get there in time?"

"In time? Do you mean to tell me that you knew he would be in trouble? That you sent me there without any guidance to do something I don't even understand?"

"I had to rely on your gifts, dear. You're so much stronger than I was. I didn't want to push you in the wrong direction. I knew Silas would guide you."

For the first time in my brief relationship with my grandmother, I'm furious. "Grams, do you know what could've happened if I had waited just thirty minutes longer to visit him? Or if I hadn't understood what to do? He was in dire straits; this isn't some board game where winning doesn't matter. If we lose Silas . . ."

Twiggy steps into my eye line and shivers uncontrollably as she moves through Isadora's ghost. "Hey, doll, Silas and your Grams are as close as two people could ever be. She may not have married him, but that right there should show you how much she loves him."

Sparkling ghost tears burst from my grandmother's eyes and she rushes toward me, wrapping me in the weight of her phantom hug.

I guess what Twiggy's saying is true. To a recovering alcoholic who's had five husbands and countless "special friends," a man who's been by her side for decades and never taken advantage of her emotional frailty is the truest friend she's ever known.

If this were a movie, I'd insert a montage of Grams and Silas through the years. The warmth of the collection of memories would prove Twiggy's point and convince me to forgive my Ghost-ma. I don't have that kind of time, so I'll just "cut to" forgiveness.

"Thank you, sweetheart," Grams whispers.

"I got there in time, Grams. I don't know how I knew what to do, but I did and he's all right. I didn't mean to yell at you."

Grams swipes at the flood of tears on her lovely high cheekbones and smiles warmly. "How's your quest of getting me a handkerchief in the afterlife coming along?"

I repeat the joke for Twiggy's benefit and the three of us have an oddly heartwarming chuckle.

Pyewacket appears out of nowhere and slowly twists figure eights around my ankles.

I lean down and scratch between his tufted ears. "Your curmudgeonly friend will live to argue with you another day, Pye. But no jumping out from high places and scaring him for at least a month. Understood?" I point my finger menacingly at the troublemaking caracal.

He casually sits back on his haunches and swats my finger away with one paw.

Luckily, it's a playful retort rather than a dangerous warning. I know this because he keeps his claws retracted and I keep all my flesh.

"All right, ladies, I need to apologize to Erick for standing him up at breakfast and I need to bribe him into giving me a copy of the medical examiner's report while Silas is in the hospital. Suggestions?"

"I could always tap my contact in the records office."

I'm not sure I want to unpack that offer from Twiggy, but I'm also in no position to irritate her. A ghostly snicker fills the third floor. There are certain advantages to a ghost who can hear my thoughts.

"Grams, do you have a better idea?"

"KISS always worked for me." She winks.

"Grams! I'm not going to kiss Erick. I'm not

saying I wouldn't like to, I'm just saying it's not really appropriate, and I'm not going to use my kisses as bribes."

Twiggy finds my half of this conversation delightful and guffaws loudly at my retort.

"Mitzy, I didn't say 'a kiss.' I said KISS: Keep It Simple Sweetheart." Grams shakes her ethereal head.

That's not exactly the version of that acronym that I've heard, but I'll take it. "Silas suggested a selection of pastries. What do you guys think of that idea?"

Twiggy nods.

Grams claps her phantom hands. "That's perfect. Even if he doesn't want to eat them, he can share them with the rest of the station and be the hero for the day. Either way, you make him look good and maybe he'll make you feel good."

I put up a hand to stop her from diving any deeper into that analogy. "Easy, *Isadora*. Erick isn't my special friend—"

"Yet." She giggles uncontrollably and vanishes through the wall.

"Looks like I'm headed over to Bless Choux, Twiggy. You need anything uptown?"

Twiggy hooks a thumb through the belt loop of her dungarees and grins. "So, you really gonna make a go of it? Here, in Pin Cherry?"

The question hits me out of left field and it takes me a minute to find the answer within my heart. "Yeah I guess, I am. I mean, at first I thought I would just check things out, probably take the cash and leave. But I've never lived anywhere like this before. It feels comfortable, you know?"

She walks away and answers without looking at me. "I gotta get back to the bookshop. Customers." She nods her severe grey pixie cut in my general direction and clomps off toward the staircase, before I can identify the deeper emotion lurking behind her bravado. But I'm starting to think she really likes me. Maybe she even thinks of me as a friend.

I take Birch Street to the patisserie to avoid walking past the diner or the sheriff's station on Main.

There's a short line at the counter of the bakery, but it gives me a chance to make my selections. I've only been here once before, with Rory Bombay, and I remember the chocolate croissant was delectable. An unwelcome thought pushes its way into my consciousness. I really hope that wasn't Rory in the building. I shove the dark idea away.

Hold on. It's not the 1920s. Girls can call boys. I step out of line and make the call.

Voicemail. Annoying. I hang up. I can't leave a message. What am I going to say? "Hey I got a weird psychic message from a charred corpse. Was it you?" Not so much. I'll let it marinate until I get a better idea.

Looks like it's my turn.

"Good morning, Mitzy. What can I get you?"

Didn't I just mention I've only been here once before? How does she know my name? "Hi. How are you?" She's not wearing a nametag, which definitely puts me at a disadvantage.

She puts one hand to her forehead and pretends to faint. "Well, I suppose I'm about as nervous as a long-tailed cat in a room full of rocking chairs, but this time of year is more stressful than Christmas!"

I honestly have no idea what she's talking about. "How's that?"

"With Valentine's Day right around the corner, I've got orders for chocolate soufflés, chocolate- and strawberry-filled galettes, chocolate macarons, opera cakes, chocolate-dipped strawberries, chocolate croissants, strawberry tarte tartin . . . I'm sure you get the idea. It's my busiest time of the year."

I recognized chocolate dipped strawberries, but the rest of her list is a mystery to me. "Yowser, you do sound busy. I'll make this quick."

"Will you be purchasing more than one item?"

"Yes."

She immediately retrieves a large pastry box with special dividers and places it on the counter.

"I'd like two chocolate croissants, a pin cherry tart, whatever that beautiful glazed thing is—"

"Oh, that's a maple oat nut scone with maple pecan glaze."

"Better make it two of those. And . . . anything else you'd recommend?"

"I'm happy to give you one of each of our top sellers, if that helps?"

"Sounds perfect. Package it up."

She carefully selects at least a dozen mouthwatering items from the case and sets them in the divided bakery box, so that each selection will be protected during transport.

Now, all I have to do is stay on my feet from Third Avenue back to the sheriff's station on Main. Good luck to me. I pay her with cash, as is the custom in this little town that technology forgot, and take slow measured steps along the sidewalk.

It's been over a week since the last big snow and the walkway is clear of precipitation, and only a few granules of ice-melting salt remain.

Right! I made it to the police station. Now, I just need to balance this box in one hand, while I open the door—

"Stand aside. Police business." Deputy Paulsen shoves her way out the front door, and a vaudeville entertainer juggling plates would be impressed by the acrobatics I perform to keep my patisserie box from a fateful fall. But despite my usual clumsiness, I somehow manage to keep it together and catch the door with my heel.

"Be careful out there, Deputy." I rush inside before she has a chance to pick up on the sarcasm in my tone.

My favorite officer occupies the front desk, and, as usual Furious Monkeys is hunched over her phone engrossed in her video game. Without taking her eyes from the screen or her fingers from the controls, she nods her head toward the swinging gate.

Once again, the comfort of familiarity embraces me. I push through the well-worn wooden gate and walk directly passed the tired old metal desks to Erick's office.

He's leaning back in his dilapidated office chair staring daggers into a report.

"Hey, Erick. I brought apology pastries."

He slowly rips his gaze away from the page, but as he looks up his focus seems to pass through me rather than on me.

"Everything all right?"

He avoids my question, drops the report face down, and stands awkwardly. "Oh thanks, Moon. Let me take that." He grabs the box and plunks it unceremoniously on his desk without so much as a peek at the delicious treats inside. "Can I walk you back to the bookshop?"

Not the response I expected. And entirely out of character. What is it that my grandmother always says? Don't count your chickens before they're hatched. That doesn't seem like the right one. It was something about a horse with presents, I think. "Sure. Is something wrong?"

He hurriedly throws on his jacket and steers me out of the station. "Does something have to be wrong for me to walk you to the bookshop?"

Now I'm extremely confused. I'm the one who flirts with him. He's the one who keeps me at arm's length and acts like he's not interested. I don't think I'm comfortable with the tables turning in this way. "It's just that you've never—"

"It's been a tough day for all of us. And you're not all that coordinated after a full night's sleep. Since you're running on no sleep, let's call it preventive maintenance. I walk you safely back to the bookshop now, and it saves me having to write a police report when you slip and fall in front of a car later." He smiles, but it's perfunctory and doesn't touch his worried blue-grey eyes.

We walk the rest of the block in silence.

His behavior has all of my senses, the regular ones and the extra ones, on high alert. Something is not right. "Was it Rory?"

In place of an answer, he pulls open the front

door of the bookstore, but instead of dropping me off, he follows me in.

I can't take it. I stop in the entryway and turn toward him. "Do you have something to tell me about the fire? Was it Rory?"

Erick avoids eye contact. "You have a back room, don't you?"

I nod, but instead of me leading him, he scoops an arm around me and hustles me into the back.

Now I feel the panic rising in my throat, and tears building up behind my eyes. I didn't know Rory all that well, but he was kind to me and maybe something was blossoming. "Erick, was it Rory?"

Erick gently pushes me into a chair and paces from the computer to the doorway, which for a man of his height takes two strides.

"We won't have positive identification on the body until the medical examiner finishes his report."

"But there was a body? I was right about the body?"

Erick mumbles, "Unfortunately."

"Seriously, what is going on?"

"I followed up on your hunch. We looked into the records and discovered that the building changed hands in early January."

"That makes sense. I told you Rory was looking around there with a realtor in December."

"I'm sure he was. But he didn't buy the building."

"What are you saying? Who bought the building?"

He leans down and speaks to me as though I'm a five-year-old child. "I just want to remind you that we don't know anything for sure. The ME won't finish his report for at least a day, possibly two. The body was very badly— Identification is gonna be difficult."

My chest constricts. I can barely take in enough air to ask my question. "Who owns the building, Erick?"

"The building was purchased by the Duncan Restorative Justice Foundation."

I look up at him and hot tears spring to my eyes. "What are you saying?"

"The building belongs to your father, Mitzy. Jacob bought the building in January."

Chills spread across my skin and I definitely can't breathe. Erick kneels down and puts a hand on my shoulder. "There's no reason to believe it was him."

"Where's my phone? I need my phone. I need to call my dad." I run my hands over my pockets, but I'm unable to focus. "Where is my blasted phone?"

Erick puts a firm hand on each of my shoulders. His face is only inches from mine.

The alley door slams.

My heart stops.

The words I hear do not come out of Erick's mouth.

"Mitzy! There you are!"

For a moment I worry that my clairaudient powers might be sending me a message from beyond, but as I look toward the sound I see the most amazing thing . . . "Dad!"

CHAPTER 6

After a proper reunion, a good night's sleep, and undeniable proof it wasn't my father's body in the fire next door, I'm over the moon. No pun intended. All my years in the foster care system helped me create a nice, thick protective shell. I never let anyone in and I didn't let any of my real emotions out. But when I got to this strange little town and came face-to-face with the ghost of my father's mother . . . Shell. Cracked.

I mean, a part of me was definitely terrified by the discovery of a Ghost-ma and a father, but now that they've seeped into that crack and filled my heart, these new feelings are something I don't ever want to lose again.

Unfortunately for Erick's investigation, the happy news fails to deactivate my natural nosiness.

I'm super happy my dad is alive, but now that I know he's the owner of the burned building, I'm obsessed with uncovering the identity of the body.

Did I forget to mention my dad is an ex-con?

He was *friends* with a pretty bad seed back in the day, and my father and his crappy fake friend committed one of the biggest robberies in the history of almost-Canada.

He served his time and paid his debt to society, but there are definitely folks who still judge him for his misspent youth. The last thing I need is someone trying to pin any of this on him. And since my first attempt to bribe Erick into giving me some details about the fire failed miserably, I'm off to try again. As I trudge along Main Street, I look up and smile at the bright blue above that reminds me for a moment of Arizona skies. Of course, snow in Sedona falls once or twice a year and lasts for less than twelve hours. The drifts around here are eight to ten feet high and show no sign of melting anytime soon.

THUNK!

As I tumble toward the snowdrift I was so recently admiring, I scold myself for not watching where I was going.

Strong hands grab me and pull me to my feet, far too near the deliciousness that is Sheriff Erick Harper.

"Well, hello again, Erick."

"That's Sheriff Harper, Miss Moon."

"You're definitely getting better at this. There wasn't even any inappropriate touching on that rescue." I try to let my enigmatic smile tell him how much I regret that. On previous occasions when I've tripped and fallen on him, his attempts to save me always involved a little "accidental boob graze," which was sadly missing from today's saving. However, just the mention of it brings a healthy glow to my blond hero's cheeks.

Erick smiles self-consciously and nods his head as he attempts a side step.

But before he can get past me, I grab his arm. "Hey, I owe you a 'thank you' meal, remember? How about you join me at Odell's for an early lunch?"

For a moment his face looks like he'll definitely decline, but then my little psychic senses get all tingly and I feel his energy shift.

"All right, Moon. But I have to run over to City Hall. Swing by the station in about half an hour. I should be able to slip away for a quick meal."

"I promise it'll be quick. Odell is probably already making our order."

We both look into the window of Myrtle's Diner and chuckle. Odell has quite a reputation for knowing what his patrons want before they order.

I'm not sure if that includes before they even enter, but I wouldn't put it past him.

I bide my time at Rex's drugstore, perusing the Valentine's Day cards and toying with the idea of sending one to Erick. Maybe one to Erick and one to Rory—just to play the odds.

I'll let that idea steep for a day or two. The thought forces me to send a vague text to Rory, only to be rewarded with—nothing.

Inside the sheriff's station, Furious Monkeys has abandoned her post, so I invite myself behind the counter and make a beeline for Erick's office. Unfortunately, luck is not on my side today, and the ever pudgy, ever angry, gun-caressing Deputy Paulsen intercepts my trajectory.

"Where d'you think you're going, Moon?"

"I'm here to see Er— Sheriff Harper."

Deputy Paulsen's troublesome little hand rests twitchingly on the handle of her gun. "That so?"

I'm not exactly sure how to respond. It is, in fact, so, but I feel that if I respond with the bubbling sarcastic inclination I'm feeling, it will only provoke further hostilities from the deputy. "Is he in?"

Before Deputy Paulsen can continue our standoff, a most welcome sight fills the doorway behind her.

"How can I help you, Miss Moon? Is it time for brunch already?"

I'm so shocked by the realization that this might actually happen, for the first time in a long time, I can't speak. However, the look of horror and revulsion that washes over the face of Deputy Paulsen helps me find my voice. "It absolutely is, Erick."

His lovely broad shoulders and delightful blue eyes temporarily disappear from sight, giving me a tiny cardiac infarction of worry, but when he returns with his jacket, I'm all smiles.

"I'll be back after lunch, Paulsen."

Her jaw hangs slack, and I'm unable to stop myself. "Was that a big 10-4, Paulsen?"

Anger swirls up in her eyes, but Erick sweeps me out the front door before she can find a retort.

We hurry to the diner through the frosty air that holds onto my breath like a living thing.

Erick holds the door open for me when we reach the diner, and I have to admit that in spite of my fierce independence, I'm kind of a sucker for chivalry.

I walk in and stomp off my boots on the floor mat, as I look to the orders-up window to greet Odell.

His spatula stops in mid-salute when he catches sight of Erick.

I wink.

He raises an eyebrow and throws his grin and his attention firmly toward the grill.

Slipping into a booth, I nervously organize the sugar packets. By color, if you're wondering.

Erick takes off his coat and slides onto the red-vinyl bench seat opposite mine. He taps his fingers nervously and looks around the restaurant like he's casing the joint.

I blurt out a random query. "So, do you have any brothers or sisters?"

"Nope. Just me."

Looks like he plans to make this more difficult than a criminal interrogation. Well, I have a few tools that he doesn't know about. I glance at my mood ring, which offers no help. So I take a deep breath and pay careful attention to any and all messages I receive, as I ask my next question. "Does your mother live in town?"

"She does." He cracks his knuckles.

"Are you two close?"

His dancing eyes fall firmly on my face and a flash of deeply buried pain surfaces for a moment before he closes himself off. He swallows hard, but doesn't answer.

"Hey, Erick, I'm not trying to pry. I lost my mom when I was eleven, you know. So, my question is more about what it must be like to still have your mom around rather than some psychological evaluation of sons who are close to their mothers."

"I'm sorry about your mom, Mitzy." He picks

up his napkin and polishes his clean knife as he continues. "My mom and I are very close. Truth is, my dad ran out on her before my fifth birthday. I never ask her to delve into the details of what went wrong. I just did my best to be a good son and take care of her."

I force myself to keep the tone light. "I'm sure she really appreciates that, Erick. You seem like a very good son."

His shoulders relax and a soft smile curves one corner of his mouth. "I might as well tell you, I bought her a house after I got out of the Army. I live in the house too. So, it's true what people say, I still live with my mom." He shrugs as though it means nothing. But extra-sensory gifts detect a strange pulse of desperation and insecurity that I've never previously associated with Sheriff Harper.

Before I can stop myself, I reach across the table and put my hand on top of his. "Family is the most important thing. Trust me. I know what I'm talking about."

He pulls his hand away self-consciously as Tally sets our plates on the table.

She gives me a surreptitious wink.

"Thanks, Tally. Looks delicious as always."

Erick clears his throat and fidgets in his seat as he adds, "Give my compliments to the chef."

Tally grins broadly and replies, "Sure thing, Sheriff." And then she hurries back to the kitchen.

We both take our food very seriously, and he digs into his meatloaf and mashed potatoes with a side of pickled beets. *Ew.* While I enjoy my usual. My touchstone. My comforting routine.

By the time he's sopping up the last bits of gravy with his biscuit, and I'm licking the french fry salt off my fingers, Odell comes out to add his two cents to our rendezvous.

"I'm sure glad to see you've decided this fine, upstanding young lady is more deserving of lunch than arrest, Sheriff." Odell chuckles loudly.

Erick tries to pay the tab, but Odell refuses.

"Your money's no good here, Sheriff. And I've got this one on the 'free burgers and fries for life' plan. It's on the house." Odell raps his knuckles on the table twice and saunters back into the kitchen.

"I better get back to the station, Mitzy. Thank you for lunch."

I nod. "Maybe next time you'll give me a little more to work with in the way of conversation?"

He chuckles and sighs. "Never been a fan of bad news. When I was looking over the deputy's report about the property and worrying that the body we found inside the ruins could be your dad . . . Well, let's just say the unholy epitaphs racing through my brain aren't the kind of things you say in front of a lady." His blue eyes light up with genuine warmth.

I think he called me a "lady." My tummy is quite tingly. "Maybe we can do this again sometime," I offer.

He slides out of the booth, stretches his arm back to put on his jacket and, despite my best efforts, my eyes dip down just in case his shirt comes untucked and I finally get a peek at those abs.

He pretends not to notice as he zips up his coat. "Thanks again, Odell." He gives the cook a genuine salute, and for the first time I make the connection that they both served in the Army. Decades apart, of course, but Odell might outrank the sheriff.

I'm not sure why this thought pleases me so greatly, but it really does.

By the time I slide myself out of that booth, I'm grinning like a fool. I wave to Odell and head to the front door, behind Erick, as is my preference. He stops and holds the door for me once more. I blush, but stop in my tracks when my mobile rings.

"I better take this. It's Silas." I attempt an apologetic gaze.

Erick nods. "Of course. Give him my best."

CHAPTER 7

I WANDER BACK to a booth in the diner as I answer my phone. Silas needs a book from my Rare Books Loft and says it is "needed most urgently." I choose to interpret that as after one more cup of soul-nourishing coffee—and possibly a cinnamon roll.

The weather has taken an unpleasant turn, and the locals assure me that the worst storm of the season is brewing. One of the old timers at the diner even says it will be worse than the storm of '84. Which is apparently the storm by which all others are measured.

While "snow chat" is new, I have to admit it's not a fresh idea to talk about weather. Back in Arizona, in my last job as a belligerent barista at the Hot Kafka, I overheard my nauseatingly chatty manager discussing things like monsoon seasons, the heat index, and the difference between dry heat in the Southwest region versus the humidity of the Southeast, on a daily basis. I did everything within my power to avoid these types of interactions. But that was old Mitzy. Going nowhere Mitzy. Dead-end Mitzy.

History has since revealed that the people I called my friends back then have ceased to be part of my life. Not that I made any terribly huge gestures to keep in touch. I mean, I did stop paying my cell phone bill, and even though my father convinced me to take care of all my outstanding debts after I tripped and fell into a life of wealth and comfort, I chose to get a new cell phone number when I landed in Pin Cherry, rather than reactivate my old mobile number. So, not a lot of crossover from the old life to the new. But I honestly can't say I have any regrets.

I'm discovering something very freeing in my fresh start. I'm not sure how many fresh starts you get in life, but since this is the only one I've ever gotten, I'd rather not waste it.

Which means, I'm going to enjoy the local *flavor* at Myrtle's Diner for a few more minutes. And I'm also going to entertain my new habit of reading the paper.

I pick up the folded newspaper abandoned on the next table.

By the time I smooth it flat on the silver-flecked white tabletop, Tally has already poured my coffee.

I lift my mug and smile warmly as she hurries off to refill the other regulars.

No surprise, the top story is the body found in the charred rubble next to the Bell, Book & Candle. The photo that accompanies the story is haunting. Not for the first time, I have to admire the careful yet artistic eye of young photojournalist Quince Knudsen.

Tally carefully slides my cinnamon roll onto the table without disturbing my newspaper. The woman is in her early sixties, but her energy and professionalism surpasses many of the twenty-somethings I worked with in the food service industry. She's found her thing and she's amazing at it. She enjoys it. And working seems to lift her spirits rather than wear her down.

I raise my breakfasty treat in appreciation to the chef as I dive into the frosted delight. I tried manners on for size, and they just don't seem to fit. I love eating. I love eating fast. Slowing down the process doesn't provide any additional enjoyment. Although, I do continue to scan the article as I wolf down the swirls of dough.

The piece delves into the history of the building

that originally served as the stables and sleeping quarters for the brewery that my grandmother purchased and converted into a bookshop. The Pin Cherry Historical Society will view the site to ascertain if any part of the structure can be salvaged. There's a brief reference to the Duncan Restorative Justice Foundation and a photo of the building's owner, Jacob Duncan. Shockingly, his fifteen-year stint in the state penitentiary has been omitted from the article. However, the discovery of a long-lost daughter and the ruckus she's caused since moving to town fills a solid three to four column inches.

I smile at a brief reference to the late Isadora Duncan, Mr. Duncan's mother and local celebrity. I might just take this paper back to the bookshop. I think Grams would get a real kick out of this article. My post-breakfast treat has nearly disappeared, and I'm finishing up my second cup of coffee when Odell slips out from the kitchen.

He leans on the counter and the lines in his face seem deeper than usual today.

"Any word on that body?"

"Not yet. Erick said it was pretty badly burned and would take the ME at least a couple of days to identify. I'm hoping to get a copy of that report today, but I have to take some things to Silas over at the hospital first."

Odell leans down and whispers, "What were

you and Willoughby doin' out there in the snow, anyways?"

Of all the options at my disposal the truth seems the least likely candidate at this juncture. "What do you mean?"

"You don't have to tell me if you don't want to, kid. But I opened up the diner that night so you'd have a place to wait for the 'all clear' from the fire department, but you never showed. And then I heard about Willoughby getting carted off in the meat wagon—"

"Erick thought it was probably smoke inhalation."

Odell stands and exhales. "You'll tell me when you're ready."

He's a good guy and I know he's trustworthy. I don't enjoy keeping things from him. But Silas's story isn't mine to tell.

I tuck the newspaper under one arm and wave to Odell and Tally before I head back to the bookshop to retrieve the item Silas requested and take it over to the hospital.

Fortunately, Silas has been moved out of the psych ward and is recovering "restraint free" in a normal hospital bed.

"Ah, Mitzy, it's so good of you to make the trip."

"I think it's safe to say I owe you more than a couple of favors."

Silas chuckles and his cheeks redden while his jowls shake.

I hand him the book he requested and he grips it with one hand while the other lovingly traces the gold letters on the spine. "At last, *Anthroposophia Theomagica*. The final piece."

I slide a chair closer to the bed and sit down. "What's so special about this book?"

Silas sets the book in his lap and carefully adjusts first his pillows and then the angle of his bed before he replies. "I have mentioned to you, on previous occasions, that alchemy is a delicate balance. Matter can be shifted from one state to another, but it can never truly be destroyed."

I quietly ponder the shifting matter that went from my human grandmother to my current Ghostma and, for the first time, I feel that I might actually begin to understand the careful magics, for lack of a better word, that went in to keeping her spirit on this side of the veil. "Copy that." I nod for him to continue.

"Temporary transmutations are the simplest and require the least exchange of energy. Lengthy actions take a deeper toll."

The hairs on the back of my neck stand up unexpectedly and I shift uncomfortably in my chair.

"The energy required to hold the bookshop below the point of ignition was vast. Your assistance allowed me to perform the transmutation for far longer than would have been deemed safe. A toll was extracted. Thankfully it was not permanent.

"Permanent? What does that mean? Permanent?"

"I believe it is commonly referred to as 'death.'"

The sensation that began with a few tingling hairs at the back of my neck washes over my body with such an intense chill that the muscles in my arms and legs contract convulsively. "Death? Are you saying that protecting the bookshop almost killed you?"

"Indeed."

I clutch his hand with both of mine and fight back tears. "Silas, I can't lose you."

"Fortunately, you did not."

I slump back in my chair and my shoulders sag. How can he be so serene? "I was so desperate to save Grams that it never occurred to me I could lose you in the process."

"Correction, we were both quite intent on saving Isadora."

I rub my hands over my face and exhale. "A 'thank you' doesn't feel like enough."

"I do not require your gratitude, Mitzy. Each day you spend with your grandmother is thanks enough. And each day you explore your gifts and expand your knowledge of the esoteric fills my heart with the pride of a surrogate father."

A sudden and bizarre thought pops into my head. "Do you have children, Silas?"

Heavy sadness washes over him, and his eyelids slide closed before he answers. "I was afforded many blessings in this lifetime. A child was not among them."

"I'm sorry. It's none of my business."

He continues without acknowledging my social faux pas. "There must always be balance. If I had chosen the path of family and children, perhaps I should not have discovered the deep mysteries of alchemy. Furthermore, I never would've found such true friendship as I uncovered with your grandmother, or puzzled out a way to bring her spirit to you."

I lean forward and grab his hand once more. "All of our choices brought us to this moment. I used to look at my life with nothing but regret—anger and bitterness over my mother being taken from me and an empty ache where family should've been. Ever since I arrived in Pin Cherry and learned to appreciate the aphorisms of Grams and her Alcoholics Anonymous mantras, I've come to understand what family really means. What friendship really means. Thank you for being my friend, Silas."

He reaches across with his left hand, wrinkled with age, but strong and kind, and pats my hand. “You’re welcome, Mizithra.”

I let him get away with the formal name usage because I need to escape the depth of emotion this conversation is hitting. “Well, I have to get over to the sheriff’s station and see about getting my hands on that medical examiner’s report. Do you need anything else?”

He pats the book lying on his lap and smiles. “This text will occupy the remainder of my recovery.”

“Good enough.” I stand and retrieve my mittens from the bedside table. “I’ll see you tomorrow.”

Silas chuckles. “Two things, Mitzy: a deadly storm is blowing in and you should stock up on the essentials; and secondly, I will be coming to see you tomorrow.” He pats the book meaningfully.

“Good to know. I look forward to having lunch with you at the diner. And I promise to make a trip to the Piggly Wiggly after I talk to Erick.” I’m just about to step out of the room when a sudden thought smashes unbidden into my consciousness. “Hey, I’ve got one last question for you.”

“Of course.”

“Is it possible to cheat at bingo?”

Silas laughs until little tears leak from the corners of his eyes. He wipes them away with the edge of his crisp hospital sheet and pats at his chest as he catches his breath. "Have you taken to some sort of life of crime in the last forty-eight hours?"

I shrug. "You know me. I say what's on my mind, and sometimes I forget to throw in a segue to bring everyone else up to speed. Twiggy dragged me over to the Elks Lodge because she thought Artie might be cheating at bingo. I honestly don't think Artie's cheated at anything a day in her life, but I did get a very strange sensation regarding the caller and a questionable patron."

Silas grins broadly. "A sensation. You're referring to your gifts?"

I nod.

"Anything else?"

"Not exactly. I spilled some water on the woman and when I looked at her bingo cards in the ensuing confusion, she had only placed stamps across the top margin. But she'd won twice— it just didn't make sense."

Silas smiles like the cat who's caught the canary and says, "And what do you think happened?"

Leave it to this man to answer every question with a question. I guess that's what so infuriatingly endearing about him. "My first instinct was that there was something going on between her and the caller."

Silas nods. "Indeed."

And experience has taught me that this is his answer. The only answer I will receive. I shake my head in frustration and chuckle. “Understood. I look forward to our lunch tomorrow.”

CHAPTER 8

A CALL from Silas forces me out of bed much earlier than I intended. Once I hear that he's feeling like his old self and will be discharged before lunch, the joyful emotions racing through my head prevent me from falling back to sleep.

As I sit on the edge of the bed absently scratching the sweet spot between Pyewacket's tufted ears, I struggle to remember when I had my last shower. Which is odd, because this shower actually has hot and cold running water 24-7. Now, the cold running water is nothing new, but the hot —glorious.

A haunting chuckle drifts through the bump-out wall in the corner of the apartment.

"Grams? I thought you told me ghosts can't smell."

She materializes in front of our well-hidden privacy booth, which contains an old-fashioned rotary phone, and smiles with mock innocence. "Thank heaven for small blessings."

I hurl a pillow at the apparition, but she disapparates before impact, and a fractured chuckle swirls around me.

"All right. All right." I sulk off to the bathroom. Turning on the space heater in the bathroom, I wrap myself in a thick flannel robe and stumble out of the apartment to pour Pyewacket's breakfast. The last thing I need is his caterwauling intrusion spoiling my relaxing, steaming escape.

Thin morning light barely illuminates the interior of the bookshop. Everything looks dark and grainy, like an old film noir. As I trudge down the staircase, my special gifts sense something moving in the stacks. I freeze. Pye approaches, crouches low, and slinks past me.

I feel like I can't breathe. I watch as my tan little beast silently approaches the bookcases and hunkers down. His short tail flicks with anticipation and the muscles in his haunches flex in preparation for his attack.

The silent, furry rocket launches down the aisle.

A muffled scream followed by a hiss and the

sound of boots hastily retreating toward the alley door does nothing to restore my breathing.

The metal door clangs against the frame as my four-legged hero rounds the corner. He sits back calmly, looks up at me, and nods once before saying, "Re-ooow." I'm not sure if I've heard that particular tone before, but it definitely sounded like "not in my house."

I hurry down the steps, hop over the chain, and race to lock the door.

Newsflash, this is not a door that I'll be locking anytime soon.

The metal is bent, the handle is damaged, and it looks like whoever came in used a seriously heavy-duty pry bar. I may or may not have gotten into some light breaking and entering with one of my foster brothers, and I recognize the marks.

My first thought is how long had they been in here, my second thought is what did they take, and my third thought is why the heck didn't Twiggy turn on the alarm system?

I pull out my cell phone and dial my favorite sheriff's station while I check the alarm keypad. I don't recognize the voice of the woman who answers the phone and calls herself "Dispatch," but I suppose Erick can't work twenty-four hours a day. "Good morning. I need to report a break-in."

Once she gathers all the particulars, she assures

me that an officer will be on site shortly and confirms that I am no longer in danger.

I inform her that my watch-cat has everything well in paw.

She is not amused.

I thank her and hang up before I embarrass myself further.

The LED display on the keypad is dead. That explains the lack of "alarm" in the alarm system. I'll add that to the list of things I'll need to have fixed.

Grams floats lazily down from the mezzanine and asks, "Aren't you going to take a shower?"

As I turn, a wave of emotion washes over me and I almost start to cry. "Someone was in the bookshop. Pye scared him away. But the door . . ."

Grams flies straight through me and flickers in and out as she stares at the damaged door. "Did they hurt you? Are you all right? Did you see who it was?"

"I'm fine. Honestly, Pye handled it like a champ. The guy—I think it was a guy—ran out and he didn't seem to be carrying anything."

"Where was he? In the Rare Books Loft?" Grams' shimmering face flashes with worry.

"No, he was down here, on the first floor."

She shakes her head and swirls in anxious circles. "Show me where he was."

Before I can take a single step, Pyewacket turns

and leads the way down the aisle where he attacked the intruder.

I follow dumbfounded. "Grams?"

"Yes, Mitzy, what is it?"

"Tell Pyewacket to do something else."

She seems to freeze-frame and I wonder if she's had the same realization as me?

"Do you think he can hear me?"

"No time like the present to test the theory."

Grams swirls down to the thick carpet and appears to kneel. "Can you hear me, Mr. Cuddlekins? Can my sweet little baby hear me?"

Pyewacket purrs as he rubs himself against the bookshelf.

"Try something else, Grams."

She pats her ghostly lap and verbally encourages Pyewacket to come to her.

The mysterious feline takes the most indirect route, but eventually curls up in the place where her ethereal lap seems to exist.

She scratches his head and he purrs loudly.

"I'm not sure if it's a hundred percent proven, but I'd say it's a theory that definitely deserves more exploration."

Ghostly tears are trickling down her cheeks and it warms my heart to watch those two old friends reconnect. An ominous chime sounds three times and I nearly jump out of my reindeer onesie. "What the heck is that?"

Grams casually looks over her shoulder, like it's a sound I've heard a thousand times. "That's the delivery bell on the alley door, dear."

I roll my eyes and shrug. Walking back to the busted door, I push it open only to be further annoyed when I'm met by the pudgy scowl of Deputy Paulsen, instead of the gorgeous blue eyes of my favorite sheriff.

"Dispatch said you had a B and E over here. This the point of entry?"

I'm biting my tongue so hard that the coppery taste of blood spreads across my mouth. But my usual response won't get me what I need, so it's time to get out the honey. "Thank you for coming so quickly, Deputy Paulsen. It was terrifying. I was just coming downstairs to feed the cat, and someone was in the bookshop."

"Can you describe the suspect?"

"It was still pretty dark. All I can say for sure, is that I think it was a man."

"So your official statement is that you for sure think it was a man."

Oh boy, my tongue has never been bitten so hard. "Like I said, it was pretty dark."

"So no description of height, weight, hair color, clothing, anything?"

Before I can answer, Pyewacket rubs firmly against my leg and knocks me a little off balance. But as I lean down to scold him, I see something in his mouth. I crouch and hold out my hand. "What have you got there?"

He drops a chunk of hair into my hand.

Thoroughly grossed out, but pleased, I chuckle under my breath as I stand. "If you have an evidence bag, Deputy, it looks like Pyewacket has collected a DNA sample for you."

True to form, Paulsen whips an evidence bag out of her back pocket and bags the hair. "I'll make my report and send this to the lab. We'll let you know what we find out." She turns to leave.

I pull my robe tight against the cold. "Deputy, who can I call about this door?"

"I'd start with a locksmith. Maybe your fancy grandma had someone on her payroll." Without another word, Deputy Paulsen blasts out the side door and lets it slam loudly behind her.

"Grams? Grams? What the heck did you do to Deputy Paulsen when you were alive?"

"Well, let's just say I may have backed her competition in the election." Grams winks and smirks wickedly.

"Isadora! Are you saying that you helped get Erick Harper elected?"

She shrugs her shoulders innocently. "Campaign donations are anonymous, dear."

"Wow! That explains so much. Thanks for doing everything you can to make life difficult for me in this town." I exhale loudly.

Grams crosses her arms and arches a perfectly drawn brow. "Oh, is that what I've done?" She gestures to the gorgeous three-story bookshop surrounding us before re-crossing her arms. "I've made life difficult for you?"

We share a hearty laugh as Pyewacket loudly reminds me of his imminent need to feed.

I pour him an extra portion of Fruity Puffs and then search for a local locksmith who will handle emergencies.

Looks like that shower will have to wait until after lunch.

Silas calls for a ride at 11:15 a.m. When a man with his unique talents says he'll be leaving the hospital before noon, I should have known better than to doubt him. After I pick him up and let him know that Odell has been asking after him, he suggests we avoid the diner for lunch. The thought of missing out on my favorite french fries nearly breaks my heart, but Odell clearly suspects something, and neither Silas nor I have come up with a believable cover story for the night of the fire. It's not as though we can simply say that we opted out of the safety of Myrtle's *Diner* because we were too busy keeping Myrtle Isadora's *bookshop* from burning down!

Looks like it will be another trip to Bless Choux patisserie for me.

"It is good to breathe the cool, crisp air of Pin Cherry Harbor. The antiseptic odors of the medical center, while comforting on one level, become an assault on the olfactory system once the initial dangers have passed."

I nod fervently. "I've never been a fan of hospitals."

Silas smooths his bushy grey mustache with a thumb and finger as he nods in agreement. He lifts his steaming mug of hot chocolate and says, "Here's to a long life of good health for both of us."

I raise my mug of cocoa to meet his and we clink them softly over our chocolate croissants.

There's no point denying that I am extremely pleased with Silas's suggestion that we start with dessert and see where things go. For a stodgy old lawyer, he definitely knows how to celebrate.

"So what has your lovely grandmother been getting up to in my absence?"

I shake my head. "So many things." We share a chuckle before I continue. "Actually, the most pressing news is the break-in."

Silas pulls his mug away and stares at me fiercely. "Why is this the first I'm hearing of this?"

I can't stop myself from laughing.

"What do you find so amusing, Mizithra?"

I point to my lips as I struggle to get my laughter under control. "Whip cream . . . mustache . . ."

"For mercy's sake, child." Silas lifts his napkin and carefully removes the fluffy white mass from his bristly upper-lip hair. "Now, if you have completed your antics, please explain yourself."

Having accidentally adopted one or two manners since arriving in Pin Cherry, I pause a moment to finish chewing and swallowing my bite of chocolate croissant before replying. "It was early this morning. I was headed downstairs to feed Pyewacket, and we both sensed someone in the bookshop at the same time."

Silas lifts one of his wild grey-white eyebrows and his jowls jiggle as he nods approvingly. "I am most pleased to hear that you are taking your gifts more seriously."

I press on. "Pye attacked the intruder and sent him packing. I called dispatch, and unfortunately they dispatched Deputy Paulsen. She didn't really do much investigating. Not like that should surprise any of us."

"And what was taken?"

I see the look on his face and I know he suspects

Rory Bombay of sending some emissary to pilfer one of my rare occult books. He and my grandmother have some old beef with the guy and it's seriously interfering with my attempts at a love life. I mean, the guy likes to collect antiquities. Is that a crime?

"Ahem." Silas shakes his head. "What was taken?"

Oops. I think I slipped into my own little world for a quick sec. "Nothing. I guess. I think Pye got to him before he got whatever he came for. But he disabled the alarm system and used some kind of pry bar to break in through the alley door, which bent the handle. The security company is scheduled for later today, but the locksmith came out right away. He said the damage wasn't as bad as it looked, and was able to weld on a reinforcing plate and replace the lock with a new heavy-duty, tempered-steel deadbolt." I jangle the shiny, new keys. "I have new keys and everything."

Thoroughly unimpressed, Silas asks, "And who was this intruder?"

I shrug. "It was really early. I didn't get a good look at him, but Pyewacket got a chunk of hair." I smile like a proud mother.

Silas steeples his fingers and places them under his chin. He slowly bounces his jowly chin on the tip of his pointer fingers.

Uh oh, I know this look. I'm about to get a quiz.

"And did you replay the scene?"

"What now?"

"Your gifts have more layers than you can imagine. The dim lighting may have prevented your physical eyes from collecting information, but your clairvoyant gift can certainly catalog far more than you acknowledge."

"Silas, I'm basically a complete noob. I have no idea what you're talking about."

"Noob?" Silas lowers his hands and tilts his head like a confused hound dog.

"Oh yeah, it's an online gaming term. Noob means that you're a newbie. You don't have any experience in that particular game."

"Abilities are no game, Mitzy."

My shoulders sag. "What must I do Obi Wan?" I fully expect the pop-culture reference to be lost on him and I'm on the verge of explaining myself when he breaks into hearty laughter.

Silas slaps his hand on his thigh a couple of times, as though I've made funniest joke in history. "You have your grandmother's sense of humor. A well placed reference, *minion*."

I don't have the heart to tell him that he's crossed his pop-culture streams. Instead, I get up and pay our tab. When I return to the table Silas is buttoning up his coat.

"Let us return to the Bell, Book & Candle at once."

Back at the bookshop, we are temporarily waylaid by Grams' overzealous reunion with Silas.

He wears his magicked spectacles so that he can clearly see her boundless joy, but I'm still forced to act as an interpreter since he has yet to discover a way to hear my Ghost-ma. Oh! That reminds me. "Did I tell you that we think Pye might be able to hear Grams?"

"You did not."

Pyewacket slinks across the top of one of the bookshelves behind my lawyer. His tail twitches when he sees the top of Silas's bald head.

Without so much as a blink of his heavily lidded eyes Silas says, "Robin Pyewacket Goodfellow, if you leap upon my exposed skull, I shall be forced to take another inch off your tail."

The warning is met with a soft but condescending reply. "Ree-ow."

"We have an accord."

I raise a hand to cover the smirk taking shape on my face. "Do you think he can really hear her?"

"Cats are especially attuned to things beyond the veil. This development warrants further observation. Now, direct me to your exact location during this morning's events."

I step over the "No Admittance" chain and

climb to the step where I witnessed the intruder's punishment and retreat. "I was standing right about here, and Pye ran between the stacks over there."

"Fine, fine. We'll deal with his actions later. For now, do as you're told."

Geez, he's getting a little bossy. Maybe it's a post-recovery thing.

A spectral mist swirls down the stairs. "Mitzy, respect your elders."

Grams and I share a secret chuckle at Silas's expense.

"Are you ready?"

"Yes, Sir."

He harrumphs into his mustache. "Close your eyes. Recall the feeling from the moment you recognized the unwelcome energy in the bookshop."

It only takes a split second for me to recall the breath-stealing fear that gripped my heart.

"Let the scene replay in slow motion. Do not look for anything. Allow the details beyond sight, beyond hearing, beyond feeling, to flow through you."

I sense fear, but it's not my own. There's a force behind the intruder. Something drives him. I hear heavy breathing. Pye attacks. I feel Pye's fury. His love for me. He doesn't think of himself. He only wants to protect me. I hear the man cry out and run. Where my physical eyes saw only a dim shape, the clairvoyant image shows me a man wearing a flannel coat, with a stocking cap ski mask pulled over his face. His hands are covered by leather gloves, but inside they are sweating profusely. He's out the door.

The images cease abruptly.

My knees buckle and I collapse onto the stairs.

"Mitzy! Are you all right, dear."

"I'm fine, Grams. It was intense, but I'm fine."

"Tell me."

The command from Silas compels me to share the details of my sensory vision.

"And why was he here?"

"He didn't want to be here. Something was driving him."

"But why?"

"He didn't take anything . . ."

Grams floats down the aisle where Pye exacted his vengeance. "Oh dear!"

"What? What is it?" I try to hop back over the chain to join my grandmother, but I catch my heel and fall on my face.

The familiar cackle that erupts behind me should come as no surprise.

"Twiggy! How did you get in?"

"Same way as always. Did you think you locked the door?"

After my Psychic 101 lesson and my fall from

grace, I honestly can't remember what I think I did. "Did you set the alarm last night?"

"Is the Pope Lutheran?"

I don't even know how to respond to that. Clearly the Pope isn't Lutheran, but then Twiggy does love to yank my chain. "I'm going to assume that's your version of a 'yes.' So, if you did set the alarm, then we have a bigger problem. You'll need to pick a new code after it's repaired. The intruder disabled—" Before I can continue, Grams rudely interrupts.

"Mitzy, get over here this instant! We absolutely have a bigger problem!"

I let everyone in on Grams' instructions and the three of us rush into the stacks.

Grams is hovering half-in-half-out of the floor with her head at about knee level. That sight alone is disconcerting, but when my eyes catch sight of what her fingers are pointing at—my heart nearly stops beating.

Twiggy crouches and stares at the object. "Where in tarnation did that come from?"

Silas shakes his head. "I believe we have solved the riddle of our intruder's true mission."

Twiggy stands abruptly. "Intruder?"

I point at the object with one hand and grab my phone with the other. "No one touch that." You know that scene in the movies when someone discovers a body and immediately touches the murder weapon? I definitely don't want any of them to put their fingerprints on that. "No one touch that. Understood?"

Silas and Twiggy nod.

"I'm calling Erick." I struggle to control my breathing as I make the call. "Hello. Is Sheriff Harper available?"

After I bring him up to speed on our intruder, my busted door, my most likely disabled alarm system, and what looks like some type of bloodied trophy left in my bookcase, Erick promises to be right over.

I have several extremely uneasy feelings.

Fire next door.

A body discovered in the building my father owns.

A break-in at my bookshop.

And now, what is sure to be the murder weapon on my bookshelf.

I don't need psychic powers to see where this trail of clues is meant to lead.

CHAPTER 9

It seems like I barely ended my call with Erick when a loud thumping on the front door echoes through the bookshop.

"I'll get it." Not that anyone was fighting me for the opportunity. Before I push open the thick, wooden front door, I cross my fingers and hope that this time I get the real thing and not the second-in-command.

"Good afternoon, Miss Moon."

At least part of my wish came true. I get to see the sexy blue eyes and strong, broad shoulders of my favorite sheriff, but it seems like our brief foray into first-name territory has ended. At least from his side. "Hey, Erick. Um, before I let you in, I want to make it perfectly clear that neither I nor my father had anything to do with this."

"With the big storm brewing to the north, it's colder than an icicle's bikini out here. So how about you let me in, and then you can lay down the rules." His grin is heaven.

There is virtually no chance of me saying "no" to that smile. "Fine. Come on in."

Erick steps into the bookshop and stamps the snow off his boots. "Now, what's this you say about you and your father being innocent?" He crosses his arms, but does not smile.

"Has the ME identified the body from the fire?"

Erick uncrosses his arms and lifts both hands in a gesture of confusion. "What does the medical examiner's report have to do with you and your father being innocent?"

"It's just— Follow me. I'm pretty sure I know who it was."

Erick falls in line behind me as I lead the way to the stacks.

"That would be something else, Moon. Since the ME hasn't even given us enough to call for dental records. I got Paulsen combing through recent missing-persons reports, but I'm afraid this one might go unsolved."

I stop before I reveal the item left in my bookshop. "Two things: I'm pretty sure the body in the fire was Judge Carlson; and I'm also fairly certain that he died of blunt force trauma before the attempt was made to destroy the evidence in the fire."

"George Carlson? Funny you should mention him. One of his neighbors called yesterday to complain about newspapers piling up on his front porch, and Artie called this morning to say he didn't come out to argue with her when she plowed The Pines."

Erick and I manage to say in unison, "He always comes out to argue about the windrows."

His eyes widen, and I smile knowingly. "I hear things."

"I'm well aware of all the things you hear. But that's not what concerns me." Erick nods his head toward the end of the aisle and asks, "Now, what's this thing you found?"

"About the B and E this morning . . ."

He nods affirmatively.

I continue. "I guess the guy wasn't trying to take anything. But he definitely left something." I turn and lead Erick the rest of the way down the row and point to the trophy.

There, on the bottom shelf of the "Mystery & Crime" section—irony strikes again—is the Michael J. Daggle Distinguished Service to Justice Award. A glass monolith secured to an oak base and engraved with the recipients name: Judge George K. Carlson.

Unfortunately, part of the name is obscured by dried blood.

Erick lets out a long, low whistle. He stands and shakes his head. "This is not good, Miss Moon."

"I realize that, Erick. It would seem that someone knocked off Judge Carlson with his own award, and then attempted to destroy the evidence in an arson blaze."

Silas suddenly appears at the end of the row. "Judge Carlson? Are you sure that's the name on it?"

Erick looks past me and exchanges a dangerous glance with my attorney.

I turn and stare at Silas. "What's the big deal about Judge Carlson? I mean, obviously it's a big deal that someone killed him, but you two look like you've seen a ghost."

Grams barrels in and whispers, "You're the only one who sees ghosts, dear."

"*Roger Rabbit*!" My hand over my mouth is too slow to contain my yelp.

Silas shakes his head meaningfully.

I stumble for an excuse to cover my outburst. "I think I saw a mouse."

"I better call this in. I'll need everyone to stay out of this area until the evidence is collected. And I'm afraid I'll have to ask you to close the bookstore today."

I shrug. "That's fine. I need to go to buy supplies for the big storm."

Erick puts a firm hand on my shoulder. "Just stay in Pin Cherry, all right? I'm going to have to ask you not to leave town."

I spin around, hands on hips and ask, "Erick Harper, are you going to accuse me of murder —again?"

A solemn voice speaks quietly behind me. "Judge Carlson was the presiding judge at your father's trial, Mitzy."

All the sound seems to vanish from the bookshop.

Erick is speaking into his radio. Silas is walking toward me and his lips are moving, but no information reaches my ears.

I'm in a freshly spun cocoon of pain. My dad would not do this. I know in my heart he would not do this. There has to be some mistake.

Grams swirls in between Silas and me and offers what little hope she can. "You and I both know Jacob didn't do this. And you're the only one who can prove that, sweetie. Don't lose your marbles on the two-yard line."

Normally a quip like that from Grams would bring nothing but uproarious laughter. But the thought of losing my recently discovered father breaks my heart. My knees go weak and I slowly slide my back down the bookcase, collapsing into a puddle on the thick carpet.

Silas awkwardly kneels beside me. His joints crack and he exhales that now familiar scent of pipe smoke and denture cream. He reaches his hand out and I place my hand in his. Looking directly in my eyes, he says, "You are the only positive prospect your father has at this juncture. This town has seen fit to convict him once. I fear it would take nothing more than a gentle breeze for them to repeat that judgment, and we both know a storm is brewing."

Silas grunts and groans as he gets back to his feet.

Erick reaches a hand down in my direction. "I'm sorry, Miss Moon. But I really need you to clear the crime scene. I'd appreciate it if you'd call your father and ask him to come in and answer some questions."

"Is he under arrest?"

"Not at this time. But the ME is requesting Judge Carlson's dental records, and we should have a positive ID on the body by the end of the day."

"What are you saying, Erick?"

"I'm saying it doesn't look good." He helps me to my feet and softly whispers, "I'm also saying, I'm sorry."

My heart is crumbling and his kindness only

makes it worse. "Well, I know my father's innocent and I'm going to prove it."

Erick nods. "Understood, but I still need you to clear the area."

Back upstairs, tucked behind the secret bookcase door, I hold an impromptu meeting of the Scooby gang. You would be correct in assuming that the reference was lost on both Silas and Grams. However, the knowing light in Pyewacket's eye leads me to believe he might be my sole cohort in the acknowledgment of the pop-culture icons.

"Silas, I need you to get a copy of the police report on the arson, the report on our break-in, obviously, and see what strings you can pull with the medical examiner. As much as I don't want to get a look at the body—ew—I'd really like to get a look at the body. Maybe I can get some kind of reading."

Silas nods as he puts on his bespelled spectacles and hooks the wire arms behind his large ears. He searches the room for Ghost-ma and smiles warmly when he locates the apparition.

I continue assigning duties. "Grams, I need you to get downstairs and listen in on every single thing that Erick and his team say about the case and that murder weapon."

Grams attempts to stand at attention and give me a salute, and even in my agitated state the sight of a ghost in a designer gown and a small fortune in jewels, pretending to be a cadet, brings a much needed smile to my face. "Get going! Get down there and collect all the information you can, soldier."

She giggles like a schoolgirl as she vanishes through the wall.

"Ree-ow." A gentle reminder.

It seems I've taken one of my team members for granted. "Pye, see what you can steal."

To the average passerby it may look as though my lovely caracal simply licked the back of his paw and cleaned his forehead, but I have a sneaking suspicion that Robin Pyewacket Goodfellow just gave me a salute.

"All right, skedaddle. You've got things to pilfer, my four-legged spy."

Pye darts into the closet and does not return.

I look at Silas and shrug. "Where's he going?"

Silas smiles and returns my shrug. "Pyewacket's secrets are not mine to tell."

What in the world is going on here? I do not have time for this. I stomp into the closet to give Pyewacket a piece of my mind and he's not there. The massive home for lost vintage clothing is wall-to-wall *Sex and the City* meets *Confessions of a Shopaholic*, but there is no feisty feline. I throw my hands up in the air and return to the bedroom. "He has a secret door, doesn't he? That spoiled little fur baby has his own secret door."

Silas grins, but confirms nothing.

"All right, I'm going to call my dad and try to convince him to cooperate. You get to work on those police reports. Keep me in the loop."

Silas wiggles his phone in my general direction, taps the plaster medallion above the intercom, and waits for the secret bookcase door to slide open before he leaves me to the unpleasant task of informing the heir to the Duncan railroad fortune that he's now the prime suspect in a murder.

For a moment I toy with the idea of sending a text, but in the end I put on my big-girl pants and call. "Hey, Dad, how was your day?" We exchange pleasantries as I struggle to gather my courage. "Ice fishing? Sounds interesting. Maybe next week. So, I have to tell you something and you're not gonna like it. What? No— No, it's not about a boy."

The sound of my dad's laughter melts my heart. And now I get to *break* his.

"They have a preliminary identification on the body they found in your building. And they just located the murder weapon in my bookshop."

I will spare you the stream of expletives my dad spews, but, suffice it to say, it's the first time I realize how much prison must've hardened him.

"Easy, easy, Dad. You can't come down here. There's more."

Once the tide of fatherly concern recedes, I continue, "I'll tell you how it got in the bookshop, if you let me get a word in. There was a break-in this—"

Oh boy, here he goes again. We are definitely going to have a little talk about letting people finish their sentences.

"Dad, Dad you have to let me finish."

His anxious stream of parental admonishing ends, or I should say subdues to a low grumble, and I fill him in on the particulars of the break-in and the bloody trophy planted in my bookcase. "But, believe it or not, that's not the worst part. The name on the trophy indicates that the body in the fire was most likely Judge Carlson."

I pull the phone away from my ear, expecting another stream of obscenities and objections.

There is nothing except silence.

The silence of a man who has been down this road and has had all fight beaten out of him.

"Dad?"

No reply.

Something like a low growl combined with labored breathing reaches my ear, so I know he hasn't ended the call. "Dad, I know you're worried. But I promise you, I will prove that you're innocent. Silas and Grams are helping. I'll find out who really did this. Please, trust me."

The silence on the other end of the phone worries me.

"Erick wants you to come down to the station and answer some questions. I think if you cooperate it will— Well I— It's just that— Dad, you can't run. You've done so much to turn your life around. And Grandpa Cal changed his mind about you and left you everything. If you run away now, you'll just prove everyone was right about you."

As soon as I say it, it seems too harsh. However, let's remember how many movies and TV shows I've watched. It's never good to run.

"Dad, please come down to the station and talk to Erick."

A moment of silence followed by an unsettling phrase, before the line goes dead.

I drop onto the overstuffed, scalloped-backed chair and set my phone on the antique coffee table.

His last words were, "I can't promise anything."

With the Duncan fortune at his disposal, my father can run fast and far. My little ragtag family may be gone before I know it. Once again, I'll be Mitzy Moon—an orphan.

"There aren't any prints!"

"*Father Brown*!" Looks like my pity party will have to be postponed while I wait for my heart to start beating again. "What are you talking about, Grams?"

"I was listening in, like you said, and I heard Deputy Paulsen tell Sheriff Harper that there were no prints on the trophy."

"Well, that's something." My response lacks enthusiasm.

Grams swirls down to eye level. "What's wrong, sweetheart? No fingerprints is good news isn't it?"

I shrug. "I think Dad's gonna make a run for it."

She spirals up to the ceiling in a fit of panic. "Oh dear! Oh, Jacob. Why won't he trust us?"

"Probably because no one helped him last time."

She sinks toward the floor as though her regret has physical weight. "I'll never forgive myself for losing faith in my own son. But he did rob the store, Mitzy."

I jump to my feet indignantly. "He didn't kill Judge Carlson!"

RING! RING! RING!

I grab my phone and put the call on speaker so Grams can hear what Silas has to say. "What do you have, Silas?"

"Good afternoon, Mitzy. I was unable to obtain access to the morgue, but I will have copies of the police reports and the medical examiner's findings by the end of the day. Now, you run over to Piggly

Wiggly and stock up on supplies. And I'll deliver the reports this evening, before the storm."

"All right. Thank you, Silas."

"You are most welcome. Goodbye."

"Grams, you keep an eye on things downstairs and let me know if you overhear any other juicy tidbits. I'm going to drive over to the store and get supplies before this supposedly *huge* storm hits."

"Oh, don't you make fun of a nor'easter, young lady. Back in 1984, I was snowed in for nearly a week. Living off sticks of butter and canned beets. It's no joke."

I shiver involuntarily. Ew. Canned beets. Gross.

"Beggars can't be choosers."

I point to my lips before donning my winter coat, hat, and leather gloves. I pat my coat pocket before remembering that the keys are tucked in the visor of the Jeep.

When I walk into the Piggly Wiggly, I'm forced to stop and stare in awe at the frenzy of activity. The indifferent cashier is so overwhelmed, she doesn't even have time to give me the customary "locals only" nod.

I jump out of the way just in time to avoid being struck by a speeding cart propelled by a manic mother with three kids in tow.

Quickly grabbing one of the last two remaining carts, I head for the aisle containing bottled water.

I've never had to prepare for a winter storm. Back in Arizona, we had wildfire season and flash floods. It's not really the same, but I can never shake the mantra, "Water is life."

I stock up on water, Fruity Puffs, canned chili, frozen pizza, microwave popcorn, and I grab a bag of apples to at least give the appearance that I had a nutritional plan when I walked in the door. I join the astonishingly long queue at the register and pretend to be busy on my phone as I eavesdrop on the surrounding conversations.

"They say it's going to be worse than the storm of '84."

"I went over and filled up three of my five-gallon cans with fuel for the sled this morning."

"I got Jackson to deliver two cords of wood yesterday."

"Oh, believe me, I got plenty of chocolate."

"Sure gonna put a dampener on Valentine's Day. They'll have to cancel that there 'Taste of the Town' event, eh?"

That last one strikes a chord. I never used to care about Valentine's Day. It was always a stupid couples' holiday, and since I made sure to never be in a couple, I never worried about it. My friends and I would have anti-Valentine's parties and make fun of all the girls with their cheesy greeting cards and pathetic overpriced bouquets of roses. But while I never made the mistake of assuming that I was Rory Bombay's one and only, we did have a few nice dates, and I thought maybe . . .

Some space opens up on the conveyor belt at checkout and I hastily unload my cart. I search high and low for a divider bar to place at the back of my pile of groceries, but I see no such item. On all my previous visits, I've always been the only person in the store, so it never occurred to me to search for one. I look at the groceries in front of mine on the conveyor belt and I see no such dividing bar exists between that pile of supplies and my pile of supplies, so I guess I'll play it by ear.

The cashier is sharper than she looks and seems to have the "what belongs to who" portion of checkout neatly in hand. I let my shoulders relax and prepare to complete my transaction.

On my way back to the bookshop I'm struck by the horrible realization that I forgot to buy coffee. Son of a biscuit eater. I really hope Twiggy has a backup supply. I can't face the chaos of that grocery store a second time today.

I park the Jeep and unload my bags.

The bookshop is oddly quiet after the hubbub of this morning. The only indication of the earlier law-enforcement presence is the yellow tape securing the aisle where the evidence was collected.

As I'm sliding the last four boxes of Fruity Puffs

into the cupboard, a soft thunk behind me grabs my attention.

Pyewacket sits on his powerful haunches and stares at me with unblinking superiority. At his feet rests an empty wooden letter tray from Grams' Scrabble set.

Gesturing to the gift, I ask, "And this is . . .?"

He turns and saunters into the dark recesses of the bookshop without so much as a backward glance.

I call after him, "Thank you. I'll be sure to make a note of it." As I scoop up the wooden offering, a wicked spike of energy rockets up my arm. Duly noted. Setting the letter tray on the table, I file the sensation under "things to follow up on later" and finish my pre-storm prepping.

CHAPTER 10

By morning the area around the bookshop is nearly unrecognizable. The charred remains of the building next door are buried under a thick blanket of snow. Everything looks fresh and new. The world is silent. The sun peeks through the receding clouds and sparkles like diamonds off the fresh powder covering the frozen lake. From my second-floor apartment it's difficult to say how much snow has fallen, but it would definitely be measured in feet not inches.

I head downstairs to brew a pot of coffee and pour a bowl of Pyewacket's favorite breakfast cereal.

Three chimes sound, shattering the peace of my idyllic winter wonderland snow day.

While I've learned that the fancy gonging is the

delivery doorbell next to the alleyway door, it must be malfunctioning, because it seems highly unlikely that anyone is out and about making deliveries after the "big one." There has to be more than five feet of snow blocking all the roads, and there's still no sign of a plow.

Unlocking the recently repaired door, I attempt to crack it open.

The door does not budge.

I check to make sure that I unlocked it properly and throw my hip into it. There's a fraction of movement, but it does not open.

"Hold on. I'll get a shovel," says a disembodied voice on the other side of the door.

I don't recognize the voice. And I cannot imagine who would choose *today* to make their first visit to my bookshop. But I am admittedly waiting with bated breath.

I've never shoveled feet of snow away from a wedged door, but it seems like it might take some time and effort. I choose to amuse myself with a cup of coffee while waiting for the identity of my visitor to be revealed.

Scrape crunch toss. Scrape crunch toss. I press my ear against the door and listen to the steady rhythm of the shoveling taking place on the other side. There is a numbing comfort to the feel of the cold door against my face and the steady rhythm of the metal shovel sliding into the fresh snowfall.

I sip my coffee and slip into a trance. Of course, this means that I fail to notice when the shoveling stops. This also means that when my mysterious visitor yanks the door open, I fall socks over buttons into the white powder.

Coffee splatters everywhere and freezes almost instantly. Ice-cold snow manages to dive into the collar and sleeves of my robe as the mystery man gasps and helps me to my feet. And next thing I know I'm staring into a concerned pair of warm brown eyes.

"Ma'am, are you all right? I'm so sorry. I had no idea you were leaning against the door."

I shake the snow out of my hair and attempt to brush it off my robe. But a good deal has already melted and is trickling icy rivulets down my neck and back. I jump back inside the bookshop as the snow on my socks melts into a lovely cold puddle of mush below my feet. "Can you grab my mug?"

He retrieves the empty cup, looks at the slogan —"Black Gold"—chuckles, and passes it to me. "Sure. Here you go."

"Thanks. Not my week." I gesture to the charred building across the alley.

He doesn't look at the remains but shakes his head. "Yep. Bad business."

I nod. "Well, I clearly need a change of clothes. So, why don't you tell me what brings you out in this weather and let's get you on your way."

"Are you Mizithra Achelois Moon?"

Oh no. The muscles in my stomach contract into a tight ball. Whenever someone uses my full, legal name the first thing that flashes into my mind is the day the police came to tell the babysitter that my mother had been killed. I used to say nothing good ever follows someone uttering that name, but then there was that day back in Sedona when Silas showed up. He uttered my full, legal name, and I ended up in Pin Cherry Harbor with a family, a bookshop, and a fortune. So, I take a deep breath and brace myself for whatever happens next. "Yes, I'm Mitzy."

The young man smiles. "He said you'd say that."

"I'm sorry, you have me at a bit of a disadvantage. Who is he?"

"Hang on a minute, ma'am." He walks toward some strange motorized vehicle with skis on the front and that's when I notice what's in the trailer behind.

"You're delivering flowers? How many deliveries do you have to make on that thing?"

He scoops up four bouquets and heads back in my direction. I can't even see his face as he replies,

"I only have one delivery today, ma'am. Yours." He plunks four vases down into the snow where they settle with only a slight crunch, and holds out a hand covered by a thick suede mitten.

I switch my empty mug to my left hand and grasp the cold appendage. "Thank you."

He shakes my hand vigorously. "Name's Victor Smith. I'm one of the best snowmobilers in the county. Won the Iron Sled Race six years running. Yesterday, out of the blue, I got a call to pick all this stuff up and to make sure I had whatever I needed to deliver it today regardless of how much snow fell. Well, you can bet I said 'no way José.' But then this guy just keeps adding zeros to his offer, you know? A man's gotta think about his future, so I figured it couldn't hurt to try."

At this point, most girls would be staring all googly eyed at the dozens and dozens of bouquets. But my attention is locked onto the strange "tennis rackets" strapped to the delivery boy's boots. You might think "boy" sounds patronizing, after he just referred to himself as a "man." But he can't possibly be more than eighteen. He must've won his first sled race when he was in elementary school! I can't stop staring at the tennis-racket shoes. "What's on your feet?"

He tilts his head. "This your first big storm?"

"It is."

"Well, let me get you up to speed." He points to the things on his feet. "These are called snowshoes. An indigenous peoples' invention that allows you to trek across deep snow without sinking in and getting bogged down. Over there's a snowmobile, or, more likely, 'round here folks call it a 'sled,' and it's basically a motorized dog sled." He nods.

That little snippet of conversation I heard at the grocery store about the man getting gasoline for his "sled" sure makes a lot more sense now. "All right, you've got snowshoes, a snowmobile, and a snow trailer behind your snowmobile. I get it. But who in their right mind is sending me a dozen bouquets of roses in the middle of the worst storm since 1984?"

The young man chuckles. "So you've heard folks talk about the storm of '84, eh? Let me be the first to tell you, this is nothing compared to what I've heard from my gramps about that one. Course, I wasn't around then, but I've heard more than my share of stories. That storm of '84 took a solid week to clear. Artie should have us all plowed out of this one by tomorrow. I suppose folks can celebrate Valentine's Day a day late, which is no big deal up north." He shrugs as though weather-postponed holidays are standard fare for almost-Canada. "And to be clear, I've got *twenty-one* bouquets of roses, an extremely large box of chocolates, a card, and a special present. So, if you'll give me just a sec, I'll get after it and get this unloaded for you."

I bend to collect the first of many vases and carry it inside the bookshop. I guess we'll just line them up on the floor until I come up with a better plan. Walking back to the door, which is stuck open in the snow bank, I call, "Hey, are you going to tell me who this is all from?"

"You betcha! Mr. Rory Bombay."

A rush of heat floods over my cheeks. He remembered. I can't believe Rory went to all this trouble to send flowers and chocolates. Why didn't he just get a "sled" and come himself? Before I have a chance to ask my question, Victor supplies the answer.

"Mr. Bombay said to tell you he was sure sorry he couldn't be here in person. He's in South America collecting some rare artifacts for his shop. But he didn't want you to think he'd forgotten about you on Valentine's Day, you know."

"I'm glad he didn't forget, but I'm surprised there isn't anything from the patisserie."

Victor chuckles. "Oh, I almost forgot the special present." He opens a large metal box on the front of his snow trailer and extracts a lovely pink bakery box.

I find this sight one hundred times more tantalizing than roses.

He snowshoes over and hands me the box.

"Do you need any help unloading?"

"No ma'am. With the fees this Mr. Bombay is paying, I'll unload every bit of this myself, take off my snowshoes, and bring it all inside for you too. Don't you worry about a thing. You go enjoy those pastries."

He's not going to have to tell me twice.

I push brew on the coffee machine and sit down to enjoy one of the delectable chocolate croissants. The aroma wafting from the little box brings instant salivation.

Victor makes short work of the unloading and sets the heart-shaped box of chocolates and the card on the table next to my bakery-based feast.

"I feel like I should tip you."

He waves both his hands as though he's attempting to stop a speeding car. "Absolutely not. Mr. Bombay took care of everything."

"Well, thank you, Victor. Watch you're safe out there."

His eyes dart toward the alley and he mumbles a goodbye as he closes the metal door.

I place my hand over my face. Did I really say that? I think I meant to say, "Stay warm out there" or possibly, "Watch yourself out there," but somehow the wires crossed in my just-waking-up brain. Oh well, he won't be the first or last person in Pin Cherry to think I'm a little odd.

I open the bright-red envelope and read the card from Rory.

Dearest Mitzy,
Although my work has taken me to the other side of the globe, you are never far from my thoughts. I promise to take you on a proper dinner date when I return.
Yours in absentia, Rory.

I should call and thank him.

Voicemail.

I'll just send a text. I'm not in the habit of leaving messages and I'm sure to say something stupid. My well-trained fingers tap out a thank you. "Hey, Rory, I just got a really sweet delivery from Victor. Thanks for thinking of me. I can't believe you missed the big storm. Take care."

As soon as I tap the little send arrow, I regret everything. "A sweet delivery from Victor?" Why did I say that? The delivery wasn't *from* Victor. "Missed the big storm!" Oh brother, my text game is sub par. I toy with the idea of texting a better message, but with my luck the second attempt will be worse than the first and only serve to amplify my embarrassment.

My lengthy absence from the apartment has drawn Grams' attention and she pops into the back room to see what's keeping me.

"What's going on? Where did all this come from?"

I bring her up to speed on the surprise special delivery Valentine's Day haul from Rory Bombay and she claps her little ghost hands with glee.

"Isn't that just the most thoughtful gift? And he's in South America, you say? Still keeping track of the weather and the holidays back here in little old Pin Cherry Harbor. What a thoughtful man."

For those of you who've forgotten, Grams was the founding member of the anti-Rory club. In fact, she went so far as to practically forbid me from seeing him. But after several thoughtful gifts, and a very expensive dinner at an exclusive bistro, she's apparently the Grand Marshal of his ticker-tape parade.

"I don't think I care for that implication, young lady."

I stare daggers at Grams and point to my lips. "These did not move. You are not allowed to thought-drop any old time you please. I might not be able to stop my brain from having the thoughts, but that doesn't mean they're open to your commentary."

"Oh, I see. So what you're saying is, if you want my opinion you'll ask me for it."

I take my time pouring a fresh cup of coffee before I reply. "Exactly."

Grams reaches her ethereal limbs toward the pink bakery box and I can see her scrunch up her face as she attempts to focus all her energy into her fingertips.

Before she can get her sneaky little ghost paws on my chocolate croissant, I slam the lid of the bakery box closed. "Not for you."

She "tsks" and dematerializes.

"*C'est la vie*, Isadora."

There isn't any water in the flower arrangements, which makes sense I suppose. If there had been water, it simply would've frozen. So I grab a clean glass from the cupboard and begin the laborious task of adding water to twenty-one individual vases.

With the town snowed in, I don't have much else on my "to do" list.

"Grams? Grams? Don't be mad. You have to admit, you've done a complete one-eighty with regard to Mr. Bombay."

Grams materializes right next to me and causes a sufficient enough fright that I spill some water on the floor. "Taking your revenge?"

She crosses her arms and tilts her chin as

though she were a queen. "I'm sure I don't know to what you refer."

"I *refer* to the incessant accidents caused by you popping in and out like a maniacal phantom Jack-in-the-Box." I shove another chocolate covered strawberry in my mouth and glare at her as I chew the delicious morsel.

She rushes at me and wraps her arms around me. I feel the hum of her energy surrounding me and whisper, "Is our fight over?"

"I could never fight with you, dear."

I smile and wink. "Good. Then you should be extremely supportive of this next idea."

She tilts her head and wags her finger at me. "You're always testing me."

"I'm going to change into some very warm clothes and then I'm going to poke around the rubble next door."

Panic grips her face. "Why on earth do you need to do that?"

"I thought you'd be pleased. I wanted to go over there and see if I pick up any psychic information. There won't be anyone over there today, with all the snow, and it might be my only chance to see if I can possibly get some sort of reading."

A tentative smile curls the corner of her mouth. "All right. But you better leave your phone and set a time limit. If you're not back in thirty minutes then

I'll have to call Silas. But I don't like you wandering around in this weather. If something really goes wrong . . ."

"Grams, you worry too much. I'll literally be right across the alley. You can look out the windows from the second floor and see me the whole time. I'll only be gone for twenty or thirty minutes at the most. Do we have a deal?"

"Deal."

I get bundled in layers of silk long underwear, wool socks, snow pants, sweater, super-thick down jacket, two layers of mittens (an up-north trick I recently learned), a scarf, and a stocking cap. I would've stopped several accoutrements ago, but Grams would not agree to my exploration until I met all of her outerwear demands.

I set my phone on the coffee table. "Here's the phone. I'll be back in thirty minutes. Give or take five minutes. And you can watch me through the window the whole time."

Grams swirls toward the window and surveys the snow-covered carnage next door. "All right. Once you get down there, you look up and wave at me. Promise?"

I struggle to bend in my layers and sweat beads on my forehead as I scratch Pyewacket's arched back. "You take care of Grams. I'll be back before you know it."

"Reow." Can confirm.

When I reach the bottom of the circular staircase, I don't even bother to try and negotiate the "No Admittance" chain. I unhook it and proceed out the side door, safe in the knowledge that neither Twiggy nor a single customer will be in the bookshop today.

My first step into the post-storm snow is a shocking life lesson.

Snowshoes work. Snow boots, not so much.

I struggle to right myself and dig a path with my hands across the alley. Fortunately, the snow is a very light powder and I kick and punch my way through in no time.

The thick blanket of snow covering the burned remains of the old brewery's garage, stable, and sleeping quarters makes navigation a little tricky. But I manage to fight my way inside the ruins and take several deep breaths, in an attempt to quiet my mind.

I don't feel any tingling of the hairs on the back of my neck. I don't feel any jolts of energy from the mood ring on my left hand. In fact, I don't feel, hear, or see anything above and beyond the eerie, silent white stretching in all directions. I scoot and kick my way forward through the snow when a sound catches my attention.

It could be creaking, or maybe it's more like groaning. Either way, I forgot to wave.

I turn and look up at the windows of the apartment and wave my arms at the anxious ghost shooting back and forth in front of the six-by-six panes.

She doesn't seem to notice me at first, so I step back a couple more feet, toward the center of the room. Just as she stops to wave back, the groaning sound gets louder. Before I have a chance to interpret the message—

CRASH!

There's a brief sensation of weightlessness, followed by a bone-splintering crunch.

You know that scene in the movies when the main character falls through the floorboards of an old mansion, or an ancient Egyptian tomb, or a secret Mayan cave, and they just dust themselves off and grab a pre-lit torch from the wall?

Let me assure you, another movie trope fails to deliver.

I am sprawled on the frozen earth, looking up through a gaping hole at the blue-grey sky above.

It would appear that burned out buildings are not structurally sound, and I've fallen through the floor above me into some sort of old basement. It's clearly an unfinished basement. The "floor" beneath me, while frozen solid, is just dirt. No cement or brick is visible.

Of course, the larger issue is the lack of pre-lit torches. I can only see what the daylight from above illuminates; and then, of course, there's that nasty bit of information about the bone crunching.

As I inspect my limbs, I discover that my left ankle is possibly sprained but most likely broken.

Oh, I've also just remembered that my cell phone is up in the apartment in case Grams needs to call for help.

Obviously, she saw me waving right before I disappeared. One would hope she wouldn't wait a full thirty minutes to call for help. It's times like these when I want to forget that tiny detail about no one except me being able to hear her. So if she calls Silas, and he manages to figure out what it is she needs and why she's calling . . .

I guess I'm getting ahead of myself. The fact of the matter is, if someone doesn't figure out what's going on before dark, this frozen, musty basement will become my crypt.

No matter how many layers I have on, when the sun drops and the temperature plummets . . . I may as well be an ice sculpture.

My eyes are adjusting to the creepy subterranean space, and I can see the remains of broken barrels stacked up against the wall, next to a rusty old shovel and three cases of shattered glass bottles.

I scoot toward the find, and use the shovel as a makeshift crutch.

Still no torch. The fire-operated or the battery-operated kind.

As I turn to survey my surroundings, I'm more than a little surprised to discover that the basement does not end. I mean, there's a bottom to it, and three sides. But where there should be a fourth side, there's a very large hole.

Regardless of the pain of my injury, the pain of "not knowing" propels me forward.

I hop and scrape my way toward the gaping black void. I lean my head through the opening, hoping that I haven't wandered into a bear's den, or worse, but the dimly filtered daylight reveals very few details. Once my eyes adjust further, I confirm that what I am now going to label "a tunnel" extends in two directions beyond the opening.

The throbbing ache in my ankle and a genuine fear of being lost in underground catacombs prevents me from stumbling down either path. Before I can make a list of my regrets, a shining clairvoyant image flashes before my eyes.

Two men.

Two flashlights.

One dead body.

The tactile imagery of the vision frightens me and I unwittingly put too much weight on my shattered ankle. The intense pain sends me into a blackout.

A small object lands on my chest and a rough tongue swipes across my face.

I struggle to open eyelids that are slightly frozen shut by tears, as I fight to focus and remember how I got where I am. I hear voices above.

Pyewacket licks my cheek anxiously.

"Pye? How did you get down here?" As I reach up to rub my eyes, I knock my cell phone off my chest. "You brought my cell phone down here?"

"Ree-ow." A gentle reminder of his superior abilities.

"Miss Moon? Miss Moon can you hear me?"

"Erick? Is that you?"

A soft chuckle of relief reaches my ears as he calls to what must be the rest of the rescue crew. "She's all right."

Pyewacket curls up next to me and sacrifices every bit of his warmth to keep me safe while we wait for whatever the above-the-ground people have planned.

Eventually, ladders and rescue workers and paramedics and beeping machines descend. But in the anxious moments while I consciously wait for help, this furry little demon protects me.

I imagine I'm hallucinating as a blond Norse god kneels down next to me and asks, "Are you hurt?"

If I weren't already lying in a heap on the ground, the tenderness in his voice would certainly have caused me to swoon. "I'm pretty sure my left ankle broke my fall."

Erick steps aside and the paramedics sweep in.

As they're loading me into the back of the ambulance I call out to Erick, "Please make sure Pyewacket gets back into the bookshop."

"Roger that."

CHAPTER 11

Concerned father, Jacob Duncan, is my first visitor at the hospital. He informs me that my discovery of the old prohibition smuggling tunnels under the brewery has opened up a wider suspect list. He hasn't been officially arrested, but is still a person of interest in the case. I can see the relief on his face and I would gladly break my other ankle to keep it there.

"I saw them."

Jacob grips my hand and leans toward the bed. "Saw who?"

"Before I passed out from the pain. I had a vision."

Jacob looks over his shoulder to make sure there aren't any nurses camped nearby. "What did you see?"

"Two men, with flashlights, carrying a body."

"This vision of yours didn't happen to supply a mug shot or a name, did it?"

"Unfortunately, that doesn't seem to be how my special psychic gifts work."

Jacob gestures to the cast on my left ankle. "I'm sorry you broke your leg trying to help me, but I gotta say, I'm pretty glad you found the tunnels."

"Me too. By the way, how did Erick find me? And for that matter, how did Pyewacket get out of the bookshop with my phone?"

My dad laughs and shakes his head. "I may not be able to speak to Isadora's ghost, but I'd be a fool to steal her thunder!"

"Great. So you're telling me I have to wait until I get out of this place to hear the juicy details? Speaking of . . ."

Jacob stands and runs a hand through his white-blond hair. "Let me go see what I can find out. They only kept you overnight for observation, to check for hypothermia or internal injuries." He walks out of the hospital room and I hope he returns with good news.

I'm seriously itching to get out of here and hear Grams' side of the story. I reach for my cell phone on the bedside table and call Silas. He doesn't "do" texting; it's ill-mannered. Complimentary eye roll. "Good morning, Mr. Willoughby. I was hoping you could fill me in on the rescue events yesterday."

Silas gives a nearly identical speech to the one I heard from my father moments earlier, but promises to meet me at the bookshop after I'm released from the hospital.

"All right. I'll call you once I'm out of this—What? No, looks like just the ankle. I know, I know. It was a stupid idea. Well, I'm sure I learned my lesson."

After ending the call, I make a face at my phone. Rude. Why does everyone think I'm careless? I went to the burned-out building to see if I could get some additional messages, and guess what? I discovered a whole maze of underground tunnels. Seems like my gamble paid off.

The door to the room opens and my dad walks in shaking his head. In his wake are two nurses and a doctor.

"Miss Moon, we'd like to keep you for a few more hours, perhaps even one more night—"

"Let me stop you right there. I'm fine. I didn't even fall that far, and I never lost consciousness." Between you and me, that's a tiny fib. But the fall didn't cause me to lose consciousness, it was the pain. Maybe that's a technicality, but I'm gonna run with it.

"We understand you'd like to get home, but

your father tells us you live alone in a second-story apartment. It may be best if you remain at this facility, until we can confirm there are no complications, and arrange for home care."

Now, I haven't had money for very long. And my years in the foster system taught me that trips to the hospital are a luxury. I feel confident in assuming people with broken limbs figure out how to take care of themselves. I mean, I've seen people on crutches. They manage. "I'll be fine. I'm stronger than I look, and this won't be my first time on crutches." Another slight bending of the truth. The last time I was on crutches was with foster family number seven. I didn't break anything, but my foster sister did, and when she was lying on the couch "recovering," I would steal her crutches and race around the house, driving my foster mother insane. She did say that someday I'd break a leg and it wouldn't be so funny. Ta dah.

Before I can stretch any more truths or make any more snappy comebacks, my father steps in. "I'm happy to stay with Mitzy until she's comfortable on the crutches. You can release her into my care if that makes you feel better. But I've seen that look on her face before, and if you don't get her a set of crutches ASAP, I'm pretty sure she'll hop out of here without them."

I smile admiringly at my dad. It's nice to have

someone in my corner. I hope he's not serious about staying with me—but maybe it would be all right for a night or two.

The doctor crosses his arms and gives me a very stern look. "The nurse will collect vitals one last time, while I let the desk know you're ready to sign your discharge papers. I would encourage you to limit your activity for at least two weeks. And don't get your cast wet." He shakes his head and leaves the room in a bit of a huff.

One nurse pokes and prods at me, removing my IV and snipping off my hospital ID bracelet, while the other collects information from the many beeping machines around me.

"Dad, can you wait in the lobby while I get dressed?"

He stands and hesitates at the door. "I'm not telling you how to live your life, but I'm pretty sure your skinny jeans aren't gonna fit over that cast. Maybe one of these nice ladies can get you a pair hospital pajama pants?"

"Thanks, Dad." I'm sure he's right, but I really hope I don't see anybody I know.

Turning to the nurse disposing of the sharps, I try to keep my tone light and friendly. "Would it be possible to get some kind of wide-leg pants?"

She turns, but doesn't actually make eye contact. "Of course, Miss Moon. Right away." She shuffles out of the room before I can even say thank you.

The other nurse finishes shutting down the beeping machines and slides them against the wall.

"Excuse me, ma'am, did I do or say something awful under anesthesia?"

The other nurse, slightly older than the pajama-fetcher, turns and looks at me with more judgment than I imagine I deserve. "She doesn't have to deal with a lot of our special patients. I apologize if she offended you in any way."

Her tone hardly reeks of an apology. "I'm sorry, *special*?"

"Patients with money."

I raise my eyebrows and shake my head. "Are you saying that wealthy patients get different treatment than everyone else?"

The disdainful laughter that escapes from her mouth before she has a chance to clap her hand over it is shocking. "Um, yeah."

I sit up and swing my legs off the bed and *want* to say, "Hey, until a few months ago, I couldn't even pay my rent. So you might think it was lucky my grandmother died before I ever got to meet her, but I can assure you that money is no substitute for family. So it would be great if you could just get my crutches and drop the attitude." Of course, I don't say that. I simply say, "Wow, I had no idea.

That must be tough for you. Thanks for explaining it."

Her eyes widen in surprise and her tone softens. "I'll be right back with your crutches, Miss."

Once again, Grams' little mantra about getting more flies with honey wins the day.

I don't think I've ever been so happy to leave a hospital. I'm thinking of buying my own cast saw, just so I don't have to return in six weeks.

Back at the Bell, Book, & Candle, Grams is beside herself. She's been in the bookshop without anyone to talk to for over twenty-four hours. You'd think I'd been gone for a week!

"Well, it seems like a week to me." She swirls around me, ghost-touching my cheek and blinking back tears. "I had no idea what happened to you, no way to communicate with you, and everyone forgets to tell the ghost what actually happened!" She vanishes through the ceiling into the mezzanine as my dad unlocks the chain and takes one of my crutches.

"It's probably easier if you hold the handrail with one hand and just use a single crutch to get up. Do you want me to help you?"

"Thanks. I have to learn to manage on my own, right?"

The hurt in my father's eyes hits me in the gut. I

hadn't meant the comment in the way that he took it. "Sorry."

"You're not the one who should be sorry, Mitzy. I should have done things differently. I didn't. I can't change the past, but I'm going to sleep on the couch in your apartment and help you for as long as you need. No argument. All right?"

I nod and smile. "No argument."

As my secret bookcase door slides open, I'm overwhelmed by the scent of roses. All the vases of flowers from Rory and the box of delicious treats from the patisserie are sitting on the coffee table.

"Welcome home!" shouts Grams.

Jacob must have called Silas while I was getting dressed at the hospital. He adds his voice to the welcome and now I have to blink back tears.

"Thanks, guys. But before anyone asks me any questions or causes any further distractions. I have to hear the story. Grams, how did Pye get out of the bookshop, and why did he bring me my phone?"

Pyewacket yawns loudly as he stretches across the thick down comforter on my four-poster bed and lifts his head for a moment to acknowledge his role in my rescue.

"When I saw you fall, my heart just stopped."

I chuckle, but I'm too interested in hearing the story to interrupt and point out the obvious fact that her heart—

"I went to the phone that you'd left on the coffee table and I called Silas. Of course, he can't hear me! So he keeps asking, 'Mitzy? Is that you, Mitzy? What's wrong?' And eventually he hangs up."

I prop my throbbing foot up on the coffee table. "So then what?"

"I called him right back. And this time as he was going through his list of inquiries, I just told Pyewacket, 'You have to tell him. You have to let him know Mitzy's in trouble.' I really think Mr. Cuddlekins can hear me now."

I glance over at the regal, tan fiend occupying my entire bed and chuckle. "And did Pyewacket tell him?"

Silas recognizes where she's at in the story and chuckles. "Oh, he told me. I've never been so firmly admonished by a feline in my life. I deduced immediately something was wrong. And I phoned the sheriff's station to report my suspicions."

"But you were trapped at your house by the storm. Didn't they wonder how you knew I was in trouble?"

"Indeed. That's when I fabricated a little story regarding a snow-storm-related accident, and you calling me for guidance. I confirmed my snowbound situation, and since I was unable to respond personally, I chose to notify the authorities."

I slap my leg and instantly wince as a sharp pain shoots through my busted ankle. “That’s why Pyewacket brought me my phone! To complete the ruse that I’d called Silas. Nice work.”

Grams claps her lovely ghost hands. “Wasn’t it genius? That was my idea. Pye and I went downstairs, and I used all the energy I could possibly muster to turn the handle. Then he took your cell phone in his sweet little mouth, pushed the door open, and jumped out into the snow. He’s a hero!”

Grams and that cat. What a team. “But, how did Erick know where to find me?”

“Well, Pyewacket and I didn’t come up with that brilliant part of the plan until we heard the sirens.”

I glance over at the sleeping caracal. “You led them right to me.”

My dad pats me on the back and looks lovingly at Pye. “Looks like that cat saved your life again.”

“It is becoming a bit of a habit.” Silas chuckles at my expense.

She flutters down to get my attention. “I was watching from the upstairs window. I saw Pyewacket tear across the alley and leap into that hole. Erick followed, far more cautiously than you, I might add. And you must’ve said something because when he stood up, I could see the relief on his face from the second floor." Little phantom tears spring to the corner of Grams' eyes.

"Well, Pye kept me safe and warm until the paramedics arrived. All in all, it was a pretty great rescue effort."

Silas smooths his bushy mustache with a thumb and forefinger. "And let us all now swear an oath not to make a habit of it."

Grams and Jacob reply in unison, "Hear! Hear!"

I shrug. "I'll do my best."

CHAPTER 12

Having broken a grand total of one bone in my body, prior to my recent ankle incident, I guess I've been taking my four functioning limbs for granted. Two unbroken ankles come in handy when you live in a second-story apartment accessible only by stairs. However, I do have to give my dad "props" for convincing Twiggy that the "No Admittance" chain could remain unhooked for the balance of my recovery.

Of course, Twiggy agreed only after obtaining a sandwich-board sign indicating, in large red letters, that the Rare Books Loft is for authorized personnel only.

Gosh, I hope our five customers this week aren't offended.

On the topic of customers, it's a good thing that the bookshop was only a hobby for Grams and not a source of income. We might have an occasional flurry of business during the Pin Cherry Festival or a variety of other tourist-attracting events up north, but in the cold heart of winter, when only the locals roam the streets, we're barely selling enough books to keep Pyewacket in Fruity Puffs.

Looks like I've uncovered yet another benefit to being the heir of a wealthy divorcée.

"I should say so." Grams swirls in suddenly and does her best to scare the bejeezus out of me, but I've discovered a very handy use for my crutches. I call it "tripoding"—having two extra legs on the floor gives me a whole new level of fright-resistant balance.

"Good thing you married well." I clutch my stomach as I laugh. "Repeatedly."

"Are you implying that I married for money?" Her ghostly features swirl with shock.

"I'm not wrong." I grin and flash my eyebrows.

Grams shrugs her designer-gown-clad shoulders. "That doesn't make you right."

Touché.

"So how do you suppose I'm going to get myself back down into those tunnels with this dumb cast and these stupid crutches?"

Grams' ghostly shriek chills my blood and I nearly lose my balance in spite of my new skill as a three-legged beast.

"Under no circumstances are you going back into those tunnels!"

I definitely can't hold a straight face for more than a second. "JK, Grams."

"Why Jake, dear?"

"Not Jake, 'JK.' It means just kidding. It'll be much easier for me to pry the information from Erick."

"No time like the present." Grams smirks as a loud knock on the front door interrupts my retort.

I hobble to the entrance and unlock the tumblers. "It's open."

The door pushes open a sliver, and Erick's concerned voice asks, "Are you all clear? You and I don't have the best track record for keeping you on your feet. And since you've only got one leg left, I thought I should double check."

While he chuckles at his own joke, I suddenly have a very different image of he and I "not on our" feet. By the time he steps through the doorway, my cheeks are bright red and the grin on my face certainly gives away my secret fantasy.

Erick holds the door open and cold air rushes in.

"Are you planning on closing that door?"

He does not. "You know, I always wondered where your grandmother got this thing? It's a fascinating bit of sculpture." Erick runs his finger along the detailed woodcarvings on my thick front door.

I've wondered the very same thing, yet somehow forgot to ask. "No idea. I'll ask—Silas." Whew! That was close. Note to self: find out about that door and stop almost talking about Grams as though she's still alive. Now, back to the gorgeous matter at hand. "Not that I don't enjoy you dropping by to see me, but what brings you to my bookshop, Erick?"

He smiles and tilts his head. "Still Sheriff Harper. I was hoping I could get your statement regarding the incident at the building next door."

"*Building* seems a tad generous." I turn and totter toward the back room, so I can elevate my leg while I endure this follow-up interrogation.

He chuckles softly behind me.

"Didn't I already tell you what happened in the ambulance?"

"Not exactly. To be honest, you were pretty evasive. I'm not saying you have a habit of being forthcoming. But when you stumble upon some clue you think I've missed, you usually gloat more."

I ease myself into a chair before I gasp with

mock surprise. "Me? Gloat? I'm not sure if I would consider being 'right' the same as gloating, Erick." I make sure to emphasize his name.

"Agree to disagree." He crosses his arm and smiles in a way that makes me want to confess all my sins. "You were about to tell me your version of the events of yesterday morning."

A sudden thought pops into my head. "Did you have to reschedule your Valentine's Day plans?"

He looks at me as though I've sprouted a second head. "What makes you think I had Valentine's Day plans?"

"Is it really that crazy? You're an attractive bachelor in a town that's not exactly spilling over with options . . . I made an assumption."

He swallows nervously, fidgets with his radio, and then brushes some imaginary lint off his pants. "No plans. You never know what's gonna happen when a big storm hits, so I like to be prepared to handle emergencies, should they arise."

I chuckle and point to my cast. "They arose."

He nods. "How about that statement?"

Erick must realize the truth is a rare butterfly that he will never capture. But I understand it's important for him to go through the motions. I take a moment to recall the details of the story Grams and Silas shared. And as I repeat their version of events, as though it is my own account, I add a little flair with a tangent about Pyewacket getting loose and me needing to track him down. I'm hoping this will explain the cat's presence outdoors after a massive snowstorm in sub-zero temperatures.

Erick's eyes glaze over and not for the first time he seems to look through, rather than at, me. "You realize things could've been much worse, don't you?" His beautiful blue-grey peepers slowly pull back into focus and the intensity of his stare makes my heart flip-flop as though it's trying to escape from my rib cage.

This is the point in the movie when the lead actress always says something brave and slightly seductive, and then they kiss.

Meanwhile, in my scenario, I nervously look away and struggle with my crutches as I attempt to get to my feet. Of course, I no longer have feet. I only have foot. Foot catches on crutch and I fall, about as ungracefully as one could, directly into Erick's waiting arms.

Erick's face flushes and his hands fumble. There may or may not be some questionable body contact.

I press my advantage. "Is this a new interrogation technique, Sheriff? Because it's working."

He shakes his head and blushes a few shades deeper as he struggles to keep me on my foot.

"Are you gonna tell me where those tunnels lead, or am I going back down there myself?"

He finally finds my balance point and steps back to catch his breath. "Miss Moon, as much as I enjoy our banter and admire your sharp eye for details. You're being officially warned to stay away from this case and especially those tunnels. There could be cave-ins, flooding, wild animals—it's not safe."

"I appreciate your concern, Erick. I'll take it under advisement."

Before he can issue any further dire warnings, our tryst is interrupted.

"Hey, doll, you want some of those bouquets brought down to the bookshop?" Twiggy clomps to a sudden halt. "Sheriff, I didn't hear you come in. Got any real leads on the fire?"

Erick sighs, but doesn't take the bait. Instead he turns my way and asks, "Bouquets? Did you have some Valentine's Day plans?"

I glare at Twiggy and she slips away with stunning silence. "Not plans, really. Rory sent some flowers to let me know he was thinking of me even though he was out of town."

"When did he leave town?" Erick tilts his head and crosses his arms.

"You'll have to take Rory off the suspect list, Erick. He's in South America. I think his alibi will check out."

Ever the curious man, Erick continues his line of questioning. "How did he manage to get flowers delivered after that storm?"

A little too defensively I retort, "Some men can be very resourceful."

His eyes darken and his hands drop to his side. His right hand brushes the pocket of his jacket and hesitates for a moment, before dangling listlessly.

I try to recover, but the damage has been done. The rest of my story tastes like cardboard in my mouth. "He hired some kid named Victor to deliver everything on his snowmobile."

A spark flickers in the sheriff's eyes. "Victor Smith?"

"That sounds right. Why?"

"His dad did a nickel in the state penitentiary in Clearwater for arson."

The hairs on the back of my neck prickle with concern. "What are you saying? You can't possibly think Rory had anything to do with that fire?"

Erick raises one eyebrow. "First you're trying to convince me that your dad is innocent and now you're defending Rory Bombay. Somebody killed Judge Carlson and somebody started that fire. Everybody can't be innocent, Moon."

"Well, my dad and Rory aren't everybody. You

better add some names to that suspect list, Sheriff Harper!"

His eyes widen in surprise when I use his proper title. He tips his head and mumbles a "see ya 'round" as he leaves the bookstore.

CHAPTER 13

As soon as the front door of the bookshop slams shut, I call a meeting. "Grams! Twiggy! Pyewacket! Team meeting. Now!"

Grams and Pye ignore my summons and I'm left with a crack team of one.

"I need answers about the fire, Judge Carlson's death, and I have to know where those prohibition tunnels lead." I briefly attempt to pace, but crutches are not conducive. "Ideas? I'm desperate. Nothing is off the table."

Twiggy chuckles. "My contact at the records office, Wayne, has been trying to get me out on another date."

I roll my eyes, but smile. "Do you think he'd give you copies of Judge Carlson's old case files? I mean, if Erick thinks my dad would kill the man out of vengeance, there's got to be some felon out there who actually would."

"Some felon?" Jacob raises an eyebrow.

Oops. So much for psychic senses. "I didn't hear you come in, Dad."

"I came in through the side door. What's this about felons and vengeance?"

"I want to take a look at the judge's old cases to see if there's anybody else who might have had a reason to come after him."

"Anybody else? You don't think I would—"

"No! Never! I'm just trying to think like Erick. First he suspected you and now he's trying to come up with a case against Rory."

Jacob shrugs. "And that's bad?"

"Dad! Just because Rory hired some ex-con's kid to deliver my roses doesn't make him a master criminal who's capable of arson."

"Who delivered your flowers?" My dad straightens to his full six feet and change and strikes an imposing frame.

"A kid named Victor Smith."

Jacob nods. "Leroy, his dad, was in Clearwater with me. He was a decent guy. Always claimed he was innocent, but that's kind of the deal of the day around there." He shrugs. "How can I help?"

"I need to find out where the tunnels lead. Can you get that info?"

He shakes his head. "Sorry, sweetie. The only people who are going to have that info are the unsavory types that I definitely should not be seen associating with."

"Right." I turn to my volunteer employee and possible friend. "Looks like you'll have to double down on that date and get your connection to spill the beans after Erick completes his search."

Twiggy nods. "I'll have to sweeten the deal. You're probably gonna have to join us at bingo—with his friend. A proper double date."

"Oh, brother. Are you serious?"

"As a heart attack. He's still miffed about you skating on our last deal with your sudden *migraine*. If I promise the double date, you gotta hold up your end, doll."

"Fine. Agreed, but not until after I clear my dad. I don't have time to waste at the Elks Lodge while I'm in the middle of a case."

"Yes, Your Highness." Twiggy fumbles a curtsy and wanders off into the stacks.

"Can I talk to you?" My dad's face is too serious, and my stomach churns.

"Are you gonna ask your girlfriend to move into the mansion?"

He chuckles. "You're always making jokes."

I shrug and crutch my way to the back room

and a chair. "All right. I'll stop guessing and let you talk. What's going on?"

"I wanted to tell you why I bought the building next door."

I nod. "To set up your restorative justice thing and help ex-cons find jobs, and stuff. Right?"

"Sure. Yes, that was part of it."

"What's the rest?"

"The Duncan estate is too much for me. It's a beautiful place, but I'm used to much more compact lodgings." He grins self-consciously.

All I can picture is a tiny cell at the state prison with a nasty metal toilet and a narrow bunk bed. "You deserve to have space, Dad."

"Maybe, maybe not. Either way, the place is worth millions and I can use the funds to help so many people. Most guys get out of the joint and fall in with their old crowd out of need, not choice. If I can help them find legitimate jobs, they won't have to return to crime to pay the bills."

"It's your choice. I'm not gonna try to stop you from selling the mansion."

"I know, but it seems like something a dad and daughter would discuss. Originally, I was planning on converting the second floor of the building next door into offices for the foundation and the third floor into living quarters."

"For convicts?" I swallow loudly.

"Just one convict."

In my mind, a little cartoon light bulb goes on over my head. "You wanted to move next door to me?"

"I missed out on twenty-one years, Mitzy. I thought if I lived next door, we could have dinners together once in a while—you know, family stuff." He shrugs. "Plus, you do tend to attract trouble like bugs to a fly strip."

"Rude!"

He laughs until little happy tears leak from the corners of his eyes. "But true."

"Possibly." I chuckle a little at my own expense. "But now the place burned down. Are you going to look for another location?"

"I can build a new structure when the investigation closes. The arsonist actually did me a favor. That building was an important historical landmark and the Pin Cherry Historical Society was really digging their heels in and refusing to approve the architect's plans for the remodel."

Placing a hand on my dad's strong arm, I say, "Don't ever repeat that. All right?"

His gaze drifts off as he replays the words in his mind. "Oh, yeah. That definitely sounds incriminating." Now it's his turn to swallow loudly.

"You think?" I laugh and rub his shoulder reassuringly. "I now you're innocent, and I know Rory's innocent, so I'm already miles ahead of the sheriff. Once Twiggy gets those old case files, I'll find a whole slew of suspects for Erick."

"You go get 'em, tiger. I gotta meet my lawyer for lunch."

"Don't you mean your girlfriend?"

"Yup. Just can't seem to get used to saying that . . ."

"You deserve to be happy, Dad. So, you go have a nice lunch with your main squeeze and I'll start assembling my murder wall."

Jacob shakes his head. "Can we call it something else?"

"Nope. I've seen more movies and televisions shows than anyone has a right to admit. No investigation is complete without a murder wall. Like it or not."

"Not." He nods. "Call me if you need anything." Jacob gives me a one-armed hug and kisses the top of my head.

My heart swells three sizes, like in that classic scene from the *Grinch.* Having a dad is way better than little orphan Mitzy ever imagined.

As soon as he leaves, I begin the slow and slightly painful ascent to my apartment. As the secret bookcase door slides open, I discover the two absentee members of my team. "Why didn't you and Pye come to my meeting?"

Grams' insubstantial eyes are filled with worry and she seems to be flickering in and out more than usual.

Pye attempts to rub against her phantom form and purrs encouragingly.

"What's wrong? Why are you fading?"

She doesn't even try to move her lips. A faint telepathic message reaches my extra perception. *I might have over-did.* She makes a feeble gesture to a pile of 3 x 5 cards and a permanent marker.

I crutch over to the pile and struggle to simultaneously balance and stoop. "Ah, Grams. You shouldn't have." Now I know why she missed the meeting.

I wanted to help clear Jacob, sweetie.

"I'll get these cards tacked up on the corkboard and you go into 'low-power mode' or whatever you need to do to recharge your spooky batteries. All right?"

There's no reply, but her flickering image vanishes.

"Meow." There's a tinge of sadness as Pyewacket calls out to his missing mistress.

"She needs some downtime, troublemaker. Why don't you see if you can help me get these cards in the right order."

I roll the huge corkboard into the middle of the room and sort through the names Grams has written on the cards. You see, I don't actually get to tack the cards to a real wall, because Twiggy doesn't want me damaging the lath and plaster. The rolling "murder wall" was her idea.

I tack "Judge Carlson" in the middle of the board and "Jacob Duncan" as far from that point as possible. If we're going to prove my dad didn't have anything to do with the murder or the arson, we have to eliminate him as a suspect.

By the time Twiggy returns from her meeting with the records tech, I've finished tying the string around the last tack on my murder wall. Unfortunately, there is a connection between my dad and Judge Carlson—and my dad and the building—and my dad and a convicted arsonist who he met in prison. It's a pretty bleak picture, and my only hope will be in that stack of case files and a fresh set of leads.

Twiggy's disembodied voice crackles over the intercom. "I've got good news and bad news. You want me to come up or are you coming down?"

I juggle my crutches to start "tripoding" toward the speaker when Twiggy's voice blasts through once again.

"Never mind. I forgot about your gimpiness. I'm on my way up."

Moments later the bookcase door slides open and Twiggy walks in with empty arms.

"Do you need help bringing the files up?"

"Nope."

"Are you gonna bring them up by yourself?"

"Nope."

"I give up. How do I get my hands on the files?"

"Like I said. I have good news and bad news. I'll give you the bad news first. It's a 'no go' on Judge Carlson's old case files. Deputy Paulsen commandeered the lot of them about an hour after the body was identified."

"Great. You said something about good news?"

"Technically, that could be considered good news. It means she's looking for a suspect besides your dad."

I roll my eyes. "Was there really good news, or is that it?"

"Wayne asked me to confirm that you're a solid 'yes' for the double date."

I roll my eyes so hard, this time I fear I may twist my optic nerve. "I, Mitzy Moon, do solemnly swear that I will go on a double date to the bingo hall with Twiggy and Wayne, and Wayne's lame old friend. And I promise not to get a migraine. Are we good?"

"We're good."

I don't care for her smirk. Irritation wells up in my throat and I gesture for her to continue.

"The good news is, he was able to get me a list of Judge Carlson's pending cases."

As soon as the word "pending" escapes Twiggy's lips, the mood ring on my left hand sparks with heat. I look down just in time to catch a vision of a gavel slamming down. "That's it. A pending case. This wasn't about a grudge at all. Judge Carlson was murdered because of a pending case." I crutch rapidly toward Twiggy. "So where's the list?"

She fishes around in the back pocket of her dungarees for far longer than I feel is necessary to search a single pocket, and finally produces two folded sheets of paper. I unfold them and begin to scan the list, hoping for some psychic sensation. "Do you recognize any of these names?"

Twiggy shakes her head and calls over her shoulder as she leaves the apartment, "Nothin' jumps out."

I plunk down on the overstuffed ottoman, clear a space between the flower vases, and elevate my leg on the coffee table as I pour over the names, waiting for some otherworldly guidance.

The list of pending cases for Judge Carlson offers a wealth of potential new suspects. But before I can target two or three prime options to casually present to Erick during my next visit to the station, the case takes a terrible turn.

CHAPTER 14

Lucky—or possibly unlucky—enough to be the recipient of my dad's one phone call, I'm now crutching it down Main Street to the sheriff's station to see what I can find out about this new evidence and, of course, bailout my dad. And I do mean "down Main Street," because, while the streets may be plowed, the sidewalks are still mostly buried. I'm counting on local drivers' winter driving expertise and the brightness of my red coat to protect me.

As I step-crutch-swing, step-crutch-swing, along the road, I smile and nod through the window when I pass Myrtle's Diner. By the time I make my way a few feet farther and prepare to cross the slippery patch where the alley meets the road, Odell jogs up to intercept me.

"After you bust your dad out, stop by the diner. I heard a couple things."

Boy, news does travel fast in a small town. I raise an eyebrow. "Things?"

Odell nods and shivers in his shirtsleeves. "I gotta get back inside. I'll see you soon."

Managing the heavy door at the front of the station with two crutches, and one broken ankle, proves to be quite a Cirque du Soleil task. Once I survive that test of coordination, I discover the front desk has been abandoned. So, I push my way through the slightly crooked swinging wooden gate, past an officer busily sorting papers and one taking a statement, and into Interrogation Room One. As I push open the door with my blessed backside, Erick and my father look up. To his credit, Erick is the first out of his chair and quickly steps over to assist me with the door.

Jacob stands and offers me his chair.

Normally, I wouldn't take it, but the treacherous trek from the bookshop has left my ankle throbbing and my patience on edge. I drop into the chair and my father takes my crutches and leans them in the corner.

"Erick, you and I both know my dad didn't do this. You may as well drop the charges right now. Judge Carlson has been on the bench for over forty years. He's certainly sent more than one man to prison."

Erick nods briefly. "Of course. But I have to go wherever the evidence takes me. And right now a lot of evidence is pointing at Jacob." He looks up at my dad, leaning against the wall, and shrugs. "I'm sorry, Jacob, but it's true. You own the building, Judge Carlson made an example of you at your trial, and now this eyewitness comes forward."

I shift in my seat and bump the metal table with my cast, sending a sharp pain shooting up from my ankle. My questions blurt out with more anger than intended. "Who is this witness? And what did they claim to witness? The two guys that brought Judge Carlson's body to that building came in through the tunnels. Was this witness just wandering around underground?"

Erick leans forward and places both hands on the interrogation table. He stares intently at me. "What makes you think two guys brought that body into the building? And while I agree that the most likely access point would've been through the tunnels, we don't have confirmation yet. What makes you so sure? Are you holding out on me, Moon?"

I lean back and take a deep breath to give myself a minute to collect my thoughts. Oops. I have once again used the messages provided by my special abilities, as fact. Time to do a slight mental backpedal. "I'm just proposing the most likely scenario, Erick. Judge Carlson was a big man. Even if he was killed somewhere else, he'd still be a lot to carry. And based on all the TV shows and movies I've watched, criminals tend to specialize. So the guy in charge of breaking into the judge's chambers and killing him probably wasn't the same guy who torched the building. One guy's the arson guy; one guy's the murder guy. It makes the most sense—"

"I'd have to agree with you, Moon." He gazes deeply into my eyes and adds, "I don't know where you got the information about where the judge was killed, though, because that hasn't been released."

I swallow quietly and launch into my performance. "If the trophy was the murder weapon, it stands to reason he kept it in his office. It was a lucky guess."

"With guesses that lucky, you should get yourself down to Decameron Downs on opening day. Seems like you could make a killing on the ponies with a skill like that."

My father and I exchange an uncomfortable glance, and my dad makes a subtle gesture with his hand indicating I need to simmer down.

When in doubt go with flippant. "Decameron Downs, you say. I'll keep that in mind. For now why don't you tell us a little bit more about this so-called witness and what they claimed to see?"

Erick takes offense at my tone, stands, and crosses his arms over his powerful and enticing chest. "A witness came forward who claims to have seen your father leaving the judge's chambers in an agitated state, the Friday before the fire."

I look at my dad. "That's crazy, right?"

He looks away, shifts his weight from one foot to the other, and clears his throat.

Well, that doesn't look good. "Dad?"

"I know it looks bad, Mitzy. But there's a perfectly legal explanation."

Erick shakes his head.

My throat tightens uncomfortably. "What were you doing in Judge Carlson's chambers, Dad?"

"I went to see him about the injunction." He looks at me with guilt bubbling from his eyes and his shoulders sag.

"Jacob, it'll be better all around if you're just up front with the information. The more you try to hide it the more guilty you look." Erick exhales and waits.

My dad wrings his hands and continues. "The Historical Society was making a lot of trouble regarding the renovations I had planned for the building. The architect had come up with a solution that would legally allow us to remove all of the original flooring and replace everything with modern-reproduction materials, versus having to repair the existing, badly damaged floorings with historically accurate materials. The Historical Society wasn't having it and they were trying to get Judge Carlson to sign an injunction to stop the construction until I completed two or three different surveys they were requiring just to delay my project—not because it was necessary."

The tone in my father's voice is definitely ramping its way up toward "angry," and if he slips up and says something about how convenient it was that the building burned down, there's not going to be enough bail money in Birch County to get him out of this station today.

"Construction projects are never easy, Dad. I totally get it. But you couldn't have been the last person to see him on Friday. I mean, someone had to see who was his next appointment that day, correct?"

Erick shakes his head. "Actually, the judge's secretary was on vacation and there's no housekeeping on Friday nights. The crew prefers to have Friday/Saturday off and come in to clean on Sunday night in preparation for the week."

"So what are you saying?"

"What I'm saying is your father is the last person to see Judge Carlson alive."

"Except for the person who actually killed him, Erick. Let's be clear about that."

"I'm not at liberty to grant wishes, Mitzy. I understand you want to believe in your father's innocence. But as of right now, he was the last person to see Judge Carlson alive. He had means, motive, and opportunity."

"So who's the eyewitness? What was this person doing at the courthouse? And what were they doing outside Judge Carlson's office?" Before Erick can answer I turn to my dad. "Did you see anyone? Was someone following you?"

Jacob shakes his head, his jaw clenches so tight I can almost hear his teeth grinding.

"She claims she was at the courthouse to pay a parking ticket and lost her way. She was searching through her purse for her phone and heard loud voices. She stepped into the alcove by the water cooler because she was afraid. The witness claims to have seen your father walk down the hallway. She recognized him from the newspaper article, that came out after the fire, about his restorative justice program. She picked Jacob's mugshot out of the book when she came in to give her statement."

My brain is whirring, and in spite of the tingling on my left finger I'm so busy trying to force a solution to the surface I'm ignoring the possible psychic message trying to get through. The tingling becomes a burning and I finally look at the ring, mostly out of irritation. I barely catch the image of a door slamming shut on a jail cell.

I refuse to believe that my father is going to jail. And if my stupid, carnival-trick ring is taking Erick's side, then it'll soon find itself in the nearest dumpster. Convicts can be rehabilitated. My dad is living proof of that. And all he wanted to do is help other— "Wait!"

Erick lifts his hands in a confused gesture. "I didn't say anything, Moon."

"You're looking at this from the wrong angle. It wasn't that my dad had an axe to grind. It's someone who has an axe to grind with my dad. Clearly a lot of effort went in to framing him. I'm willing to bet that this so-called eyewitness is connected to all of it. You're forgetting that my father was trying to set up an organization to help prisoners transition to legal employment that compensates them fairly, so they wouldn't be forced back into a life of crime."

My father's jaw relaxes a fraction and he nods stiffly.

Erick paces in front of the door. "Let's say I agree with you. What does that prove? Your father still had an argument with the victim. Your father was still the last person to see the man alive."

"The murderer was the last person to see Judge Carlson alive." I repeat my position with increased emphasis. "And you know this town better than me, Erick. Who has the most to lose if ex-cons are given legitimate employment opportunities?"

I can see the sparkle of an idea forming in Erick's eyes. If all I've managed to do is give him reasonable doubt about my father's guilt—mission accomplished. I better act quickly before I perform my usual foot in mouth gymnastics and lose whatever advantage I've gained. "I'll take care of my dad's bail. He'll be staying with me for the rest of the week. Let us know if you need anything." I struggle to my feet and my father hands me my crutches.

To my utter shock and awe, Erick opens the door of the interrogation room without any hesitation. "I'm sure I don't have to tell you not to leave town, Jacob."

"I'm not going anywhere, Sheriff."

My father and I head to the front desk and process the bail paperwork with Furious Monkeys, who, to her credit, manages to set her phone down for nearly seven minutes while she puts us through our paces.

Safely outside the sheriff's station, I stop and

lean against my father's shoulder. "You're not going down for this, Dad. I promise."

He wraps a strong arm around my shoulders and nods his head. Clenching his jaw tightly and sniffling back the emotion that threatens to spill over, he gives me a fatherly hug.

Lightening the mood with macabre humor is my specialty. "Want to head over to the diner for your last meal?"

His boisterous laughter is swallowed up in the snow banks and he shakes his head at my attempted distraction. "I can't think of a better last meal."

We secure one of the many empty booths at Myrtle's Diner and I slide my back against the wall so I can elevate my leg on the red-vinyl bench seat.

Odell gives me a spatula salute, and I hear a basket of fries plunge into bubbling oil. The day is already improving.

"What did you mean when you said who has the most to lose?" Jacob grabs a sugar packet and flicks it back and forth between his hands.

"I saw a little vision in my mood ring. It was the door of a prison cell slamming shut. But I know you're innocent, so I kind of guessed that the message must have something to do with convicts as a group, rather than just you."

A terse, humorless laugh escapes from my father's throat. "I guess I should find it comforting that I'm not the first convict that came to mind."

"Dad, you have to believe me. I know you're innocent. We can figure this out. I'm telling you, there's something to my theory. When I said 'who would have the most to lose,' I saw something in Erick's eyes and I sensed the way his energy changed. Someone came to mind."

"Pin Cherry Harbor isn't as squeaky clean as folks would like you to think."

Ooh, small-town gossip. "What do you mean?"

"You don't spend fifteen years in the state pen and not hear a lot of stories about a lot of crimes in a lot of small towns up north."

"Like what?"

Before my father can answer. Odell sidles up next to the table.

"Mind if I take a seat, Jacob?" He slides our plates on the table and my father scoots over to make room for our friend.

Smiling warmly, I ask, "You said you had something to tell me? Is it about my dad's case?"

Odell nods once and looks furtively around the diner before he leans forward and whispers as quietly as his scratchy voice allows. "Some folks are saying that Carlson had a gambling problem."

Jacob leans back and grips the edge of the silver-flecked white Formica. "Does Twiggy still know that guy at the bingo hall?"

I shake my head. "No idea, but I can ask. Why?"

My dad chews the inside of his cheek. "How do you feel about a little undercover work?"

I smile greedily. "Practice makes perfect."

Odell and Jacob laugh far too easily.

CHAPTER 15

Lucky for me, when rich young heiresses offer to host high-stakes underground Scrabble games, word travels fast.

Jacob helps me rearrange all the small oak reading tables in the Rare Books Loft and recommends that we place the antique lamps, with their fragile green glass shades, in the apartment in case things go south.

I sincerely hope things do not go south, or any other direction. I'm simply hoping to get this game on someone's radar.

Turns out, Twiggy does know someone, who knows someone. Her bingo hall contact puts us in touch with a man who'll run the game for a cut of the winnings, as their fee for connecting us with the high rollers. They also extend credit on a case-by-case basis via a representative that will attend the game to audit the proceedings and make sure our *organizer* isn't short changed.

"Grams, are you sure that we can actually cheat at Scrabble?"

"Of course, dear. You'll see. We'll play it stupid for a couple games just to draw them into some bigger bets, and then we'll clean 'em out. If you want to find out who's behind illegal gambling around here, this is the shortest route between two points."

I shrug. "Dad, you can't be here during the game." I punch his arm playfully.

He nods. "Ain't that the truth? I'll take Amaryllis out to dinner tonight and invite her back to the mansion. Sounds like the realtor's got a couple of big fish on the line for the place. Might be my last chance for a romantic evening on the lake."

"Too bad Amaryllis wasn't with you the night of the fire."

My dad tilts his head and gives me a very fatherly headshake. "Amaryllis is more to me than an alibi, Mitzy."

"I'm sure she is, Dad. I'm just saying . . ."

Twiggy clomps up the circular staircase and shakes her head. "Who's in charge of this disaster?"

"What?" I swallow loudly. "The lamps are in the apartment for safekeeping."

She makes no effort to contain her disappointment. "The tables get tucked down each arm of the narrow balconies." She gestures to the left and the right like a flight attendant pointing out the exits. "That prevents people from wandering out of sight. And it shows off the space better. Use your head." She turns around and retreats downstairs.

Clearly the "giving of instructions" and "executing of said instructions" are two different things to Twiggy.

Dad begins rearranging all the tables, and I hobble around closing the little gold caps on the floor plugs with the tip of my crutch.

"So what if our plan doesn't work and I start losing?"

Dad calls from the far end one of the narrow balconies, "If you start losing, then you better quit. If you ask them to extend you credit, you'll end up in hotter water than a missionary in a cannibal's pot."

"Dad!" I laugh at the imagery, but I'm pretty sure I don't want to be on the wrong side of some small-town loan shark.

Time to get myself ready for the event. Grams and I head into my glorious closet to find the perfect outfit for *The Sting*.

Since I have to stumble around on crutches, her usual selection of three- to five-inch heels is off the table. My happiness abounds. Eventually, she manages to polish me into her version of a spoiled little rich kid, complete with a diamond choker and an emerald ring, which was a gift from Rory.

Our guests finally arrive. Twiggy escorts three men and one woman up to the loft.

They each hand me a playing card when they reach the top of the steps.

The king of clubs. He nods and proceeds to the game table.

The king of diamonds. He steps to my side and waits.

The king of spades. As he hands me his card, he asks, "Where's the booze?"

"The server will be up before the game begins," I say with a stiff smile.

And finally, the queen of hearts. She has a massive ruby ring on her left hand and I'm sure her pearls are the real thing.

The king of diamonds pulls me aside. "No one uses their real names during these tournaments. You will be known as the queen of diamonds."

I brush the diamond choker Grams selected to accent my red cashmere sweater and chuckle. "Queen of diamonds it is."

"I'm here to monitor the game and account for the cash. All bets will be placed with me and all payouts will come from me."

I nod and smile.

"Good evening, everyone. Welcome to the Bell, Book & Candle. Please take your seats at the gaming table. I'm your hostess, the queen of diamonds." I hold my breath for a minute, waiting for the characters from the movie *Clue* to traipse out of the secret bookcase door as keystone cops' music swells. Instead—

Twiggy clambers up the steps with a small notepad and adds, "And I'm the ace of spades. Drink orders?"

The players call out their drink orders to Twiggy as they take their seats.

She disappears down the stairs and returns a short while later with the beverages.

Originally we had planned to cater the event, but the organizer insisted we keep a very low profile, with no outside staff. As a result, they get the pleasure of Twiggy's service.

A burgundy velvet bag is passed to the right. We each extract a letter.

"E."

"L."

"C."

I reach for the bag and fish around revealing my tile to the others. "B."

The king of clubs and the queen of hearts exhale.

"Beginners luck," I joke.

We all toss our letters back in and, starting with me, draw seven tiles each. I carefully arrange my tiles on my letter tray.

That's a terrible draw, Mitzy!

I jump and nearly tip my letters.

The queen of hearts immediately responds. "Everything okay over there?"

Think. Think. Think. "My ankle's not healing as fast as the doctor had hoped. I get some strange nerve pain every now and then. Generally, I take something for it, but I wanted to keep my head clear." Looks like liar-liar-pants-on-fire classes from foster sister number two paid off. Even I believed that crock of leprechaun tears. Time to get to work.

Grams swirls behind the player to my right and sends me a message. *The king of clubs has a great word. He could clear his whole board. I say we do everything we can to make that happen so you lose this first round.*

I send my telepathic reply. *Copy that.*

Grams checks out the other boards and returns to help me play the right word to get the dominoes falling in the direction we need. I could've played "TOASTER," but I play "TOAST" and call out my score to the king of diamonds.

He locks it in and nods for the next player to take their turn.

Spades plays the word we intended, as does the queen of hearts.

When the play moves to the king of clubs he fusses with his letters, moving them back and forth on his board several times. His actions and facial expressions are quite convincing.

If it weren't for my psychic gifts, I would never suspect him of bluffing.

Eventually, he feigns amazement and places all seven of his tiles on the board. He calls out his score and the additional fifty points for clearing his rack.

The other competitors nod and the next round begins.

Play is slow and measured. No one hurries to put their tiles on the board, but there are also no delays. These players clearly think several moves ahead, planning alternate locations for their words and alternate words should a more advantageous tile be played in the interim.

Without Grams' help, I would've put on an extremely poor performance. However, regardless of my ghostly advantage, or perhaps because of it, the first game goes to the king of clubs.

King of diamonds makes a notation in his ledger, the tiles are returned to the burgundy velvet bag, and we begin a new game.

This time the winner of the coveted "first word" goes to the king of spades. He places a horrible three-letter word "ZAX" in the middle of the board and the rest of us groan simultaneously.

The night wears on, letters and words flash before me while Grams zips around in the background orchestrating the best outcome for our team.

By the fourth game, I'm on my second win and the king of clubs is out of chips.

He asks everyone to cover their letters so that he may excuse himself from the table. He approaches the king of diamonds and after hushed conversation returns to the table flush with chips.

Bingo! Wrong game, but you get the idea. We have successfully activated the line of credit feature. Now we need to make absolutely sure he loses this final game.

The speed of play has increased, and not only do I see tiny beads of sweat forming on the king of clubs' temples, but I can sense a visceral fear in his energy.

Grams, I don't like where this is headed. He feels like a loose cannon.

She completely ignores my concern and replies, *Ask daddy diamonds over there if you can raise the limit.*

"Could everyone cover their tiles, please?" I excuse myself from the table and request to raise the bet per round to five thousand dollars.

The king of diamonds nods.

I return to my seat.

"The buy-in per round has been raised to five." He makes the dispassionate announcement and returns to his seat.

The king of clubs is stretched to the breaking point. He excuses himself. Returns with more chips. His hands visibly shake when he places his chips in the buy-in circle.

She swirls around the table and claps her ring-ensconced hands. *Double the bet, Mitzy.*

Grams! This poor man is gonna have a coronary in my bookstore.

If you can't stand the heat get out of the kitchen! Close the deal.

You're ruthless!

I'm a winner, young lady. There's a difference.

"Geez Louise," I accidently mumble aloud.

Queen of hearts places a perfectly manicured nail behind her multi-carat diamond earring and tilts her head my direction. "Beg your pardon?"

Oops. Time for cover story number twenty-seven. "Sorry, I think my dyslexia got the better of me. Not sure what I was thinking when I doubled the bet." I give a loud swallow to complete my ruse.

The king of clubs mops his brow. "Come on, play a word. You're slowing down the show."

Grams' ghostly snicker does nothing to ease my conscience. I carefully lay my seven letters on the board, straight through a triple word score, and grabbing an available "U" to create, QUIXOTRY. The total for the play alone is over one hundred points plus the additional fifty for clearing my rack —for the second time this game.

Grams claps her hands and sends me a message. *That's it. You're out of their reach. There aren't enough tiles left in the bag for any of them to catch you. Well played.*

Play goes around the board two more times before the king of diamonds announces the end of the tournament.

The king of clubs swipes the board onto the floor with one angry slash of his arm. He grips the table and grumbles through clenched teeth, "Something isn't right." His eyes dart wildly around the room.

My first thought is he somehow sensed the presence of my ghostly conspirator. But before I can jump to any conclusions, the king of diamonds pulls a gun.

Grams shrieks and swirls around the room frantically.

I desperately send her a message not to do anything.

"The tournament is over. Players will now leave the premises. King of clubs, you have twenty-four hours to settle your debt."

The king of clubs' knuckles whiten, and for a second I worry that he's about to flip the table over. I'm hoping he chooses one of the other two directions. I've already got a broken ankle; I don't need a smashed face.

"Something wasn't right about this game. And you better believe *she's* gonna hear about it." He turns and stalks out of the bookshop. The heavy wooden door slams shut behind him.

The king of diamonds slips his gun back into his shoulder holster. "My apologies for the king of clubs' behavior. Generally, our players are more carefully vetted. Thank you all for playing."

The queen of hearts rises and fetches her grey fox-fur-trimmed coat from the banister. "Not sure how a dyslexic on pain meds can manage such a complicated strategy. Kudos to you, queen of diamonds."

Her compliment is drenched in sarcasm. Despite my intention to make myself as unmemorable as possible, I'm sorry to say my "tough-girl" roots peek out. "And for a no talent divorcée keeping herself warm in last year's couture, you made a valiant effort." I smile and nod my head patronizingly.

Her eyes widen in shock.

And unfortunately my clairsentience receives a solid punch in the gut as I experience the pain of my own snark. Serves me right.

Grams "tsks" from above. "Honestly, that coat hasn't been in fashion since the nineties."

Leave it to Grams to set the fashion record straight.

The king of spades leaves with nothing more than an unceremonious nod.

The king of diamonds approaches and hands me a slip of paper. "You can redeem this voucher—"

The rest of his instructions are lost as my head is flooded with images. The slips of paper. The girl in the pink sweater. The bingo hall. It's all connected!

"Miss, you need to take the voucher."

"Right. Sorry. You were saying I redeem this at the bingo hall?"

"No, Miss, at the Hawk Island Casino." He raises an eyebrow and narrows his gaze.

Oops. Guess I should've listened a little more carefully.

Lucky for me, Twiggy was audience to my mistake and stomps in to my rescue. "Thanks for stopping by. Good game. Let me show you out." She hustles him down the stairs, and I hear the tumblers of the front door fall into place after he leaves.

Grams rockets towards me. "Why did you say the bingo hall? Weren't you listening to him?"

"I don't know. When I saw the slip of paper . . . It's the same as the vouchers they were giving out at the Elks Lodge. I kind of zoned out and I didn't hear what he actually said."

"Zoned out?"

"It just means—"

"I know what it means, dear. I was wondering if perhaps you were receiving a message and that's what caused your focus to slip?"

"I was. It's all connected somehow."

Twiggy calls up from the first floor. "I'm gonna head out. You better come down and set the alarm after I leave. The king of clubs looked more than a little sideways."

"Copy that." I carefully crutch my way down the stairs and lock up with more concern than ever before.

Tomorrow I'll visit Hawk Island Casino. If Judge Carlson really did have a gambling problem, maybe there'll be someone who remembers him.

CHAPTER 16

I ALWAYS THOUGHT there was nothing worse than a sore loser. Clearly sanctimonious, gloating winner runs a pretty close second. As Silas chauffeurs me out to the casino in my Jeep, after my stern refusal to freeze to death in his model-T, he lectures me on the finer points of sportsmanship.

"I understand that you and your grandmother were caught up in the moment, but you took unnecessary risk and perhaps opened yourself to discovery."

"I know. I know. I already spoke to Grams about it this morning. She told me to stick to my story about beginner's luck and definitely not mention her name."

Silas harrumphs and smooths his mustache with a thumb and finger. "Indeed."

"I feel like there's a story there. It might be better if you tell me now, rather than send me into this casino blind."

"Send you in? I have every intention of accompanying you into the casino, Mitzy."

"No. No. No. I can't waltz in there with legal representation and pretend like I'm some hack Scrabble player on a lucky streak. I plan to crutch in there in my ridiculous, wide-leg sweatpants, and put on the performance of my orphaned life."

Silas shakes his head, but does not respond. "Were you aware that Hawk Island is, in fact, not an actual island?"

"First I'm hearing it. I only found out about Hawk Island yesterday, so it's safe to assume I'm a little sketchy on details."

"The land is more accurately referred to as an isthmus, but the tribe insisted on the name for ancestral purposes. It is still a point of contention between the tribal elders and the state." He pulls up next to the curb, a fair distance from the front doors. "I acquiesce. Do you have your phone?"

I nod. "If I'm not out in thirty minutes, you should probably call somebody." I shrug and open my door.

"If you're not out in thirty minutes, I shall come in after you."

I chuckle as I get my crutches situated on the

salted sidewalk. "I suppose you're all the cavalry I really need. Thank you." I slam the door and he drives around to a parking space that gives him a good view of the entrance.

I carefully crutch my way to the front door of the garish structure, blinking my eyes against the gaudy automated neon light displays, bright even in the middle of the day. What an enormous waste of electricity.

The automatic door slides open and I search for an information desk. There's nothing but flashing lights, ding-donging machines, and the sound of tickets whizzing out of slot machines. I guess when someone hits a jackpot and coins come pouring out in a loud clatter is only a thing in the movies. It appears that modern casinos have switched over to more of a "Chuck E. Cheese" payout system.

I finally spot a middle-aged woman crammed into a teeny, tiny, low-cut waitress dress, and I approach. "Can you tell me where I can find the cashier?"

She points toward the far side of the casino, through a maze of blinking and bonging. I nod my thanks and begin my quest.

The folks posted up at the various slot machines, Keno tables, and roulette wheels, have an eerie greenish glow in the neon, windowless casino. I instantly slip into a possible student film, set during the zombie apocalypse, where walking dead prefer poker chips to brains.

My lack of focus leaves me open to attack, and I'm nearly run down by a woman piloting a Jazzy while escorted by a standard poodle on either side. I barely pull my crutch out of the way as she putters by with a furious scowl permanently emblazoned on her face.

I finally reach the promised land, announced by the bright golden marquis above the prison-barred windows. Approaching an available cashier, I present my voucher.

The woman takes the voucher without any verbal exchange. She turns to a blinking machine and scans the slip. The machine beeps in what, even to my amateur ears, sounds like a bad way. My extra senses tingle as she retrieves the slip and studies it with great care.

She turns to me and mumbles without making eye contact, "Wait here."

That does not sound good. In every movie I've ever seen, when someone is told to "Wait here," the next scene generally involves him or her either being arrested or roughed up in a dark alley. I'm choosing not to wait.

My plan to ask a few innocent questions and dig up dirt on Judge Carlson will have to be postponed. I don't particularly need the winnings, and

I'm in no condition for handcuffs or fisticuffs. I turn and crutch a return path through the flashing labyrinth with the faltering expertise of the recently one-legged.

A tall Native American man steps in front of me and I careen directly into him before I'm able to coordinate my good leg and my two aluminum ones into a safe stop.

"I'm so sorry. I didn't see you." Another two men approach from either side.

The man I crashed into trains his dark eyes on my face. "Ms. Moon?"

Even though he phrased it as a question, I get the distinct impression that he already knows the answer. "That's correct."

"She wants to see you. Follow us."

I'm not sure who "she" is, but once again his request was not framed as a question. He marches forward and I hobble along behind, flanked by the two additional enforcers.

We pass through a doorway into a long hallway that leads into a skywalk between the casino and a smaller building. I'm grateful for the glass-enclosed walkway that prevents me from having to negotiate a potentially icy sidewalk. But I also realize, I'm now out of reach of Silas's assistance. Even his alchemical transmutations don't allow him to see through walls.

My guide opens the door into a large plush office. Extremely modern decor. White leather couches, glass-and-chrome tables, and very expensive-looking art hanging on the walls.

"Welcome to Hawk Island." The large, powerful Native American woman sitting behind the birchwood desk in her crisp white suit brings instant flashes of *Fantasy Island.*

I simply nod my head for fear that if I open my mouth, I will most surely say, "The plane! The plane!"

The woman gestures to a plush white leather chair in front of her desk. I take a seat and lay my crutches on the floor.

"Thank you for coming, Ms. Moon."

Her tone of voice implies I had a choice. However, that's not the way I remember things. "And you are?"

"Where are my manners? Jimmy, get the young lady a drink, and see if her lawyer needs a hot chocolate. It must be cold in that Jeep." Her obsidian black eyes come to rest on me and I somehow feel she can see straight into my heart.

"Let me get straight to the point. Leticia Whitecloud runs the gambling in Birch County and on the Hawk Island reservation. No one moves into Leticia's territory and lives to tell the tale. You may consider this a friendly warning, and the loss of your winnings far preferable to the other options considered."

The authority she wields leads me to suspect that she is Leticia Whitecloud. Not many people talk about themselves in the third person, but Mitzy Moon feels like this might be one of those people. "Ms. Whitecloud, it was never my intention to step on anyone's toes. My grandmother was a big fan of Scrabble, and I simply wanted to host a game in her memory." I attempt to look as young and stupid as possible.

Leticia nods to one of the men standing on either side of the door and he brings two glasses of brown liquid to her desk, placing one in front of her and one in front of me. He retreats.

She raises her glass. "To the ancestors."

I pick up my glass and repeat her toast. "To the ancestors."

She throws back her drink in one fell swoop and taps the empty cup twice on the blotter on her desk.

I follow suit. However, what I thought was whiskey is clearly something else entirely. I fumble the double tap as I'm choking down the syrupy liquid.

She chuckles and her goons echo the humorless laughter. "Never had the famous Hawk Island birch vodka, eh?" She laughs in earnest now and the three men behind me match her tone.

"I can't say that I have. But I haven't been up north that long, and I enjoy learning new things, Ms. Whitecloud."

She nods her head and raises her glass for refills.

She still hasn't objected to the use of the name, so I'm going to proceed with my assumption that this is Leticia Whitecloud. I'm also going to assume that a birch vodka related hangover might be in my future. At least I don't have to concern myself with Silas getting worried. I'm sure that when he receives his hot chocolate, he'll solve the mystery of my whereabouts. A second round of birch vodka is set before us and I brace myself for impact. This time I manage the shot and the double tap, and even receive a nod from Leticia.

She leans back in her large white leather office chair. "How long have you been playing Scrabble, Ms. Moon?"

"Not long. Just beginner's luck, I guess."

Her smile fades and her features harden. "You don't run gaming as long as Leticia Whitecloud and still believe in beginner's luck. But we've all heard the stories about your grandmother. If you have her gift, Leticia Whitecloud could find well-paying work for someone like you."

Uh oh. Silas and I did not discuss this possibility. I clearly can't reveal my psychic powers, but the atmosphere in the room makes refusing her offer seem like a very bad idea. "Certainly something to consider."

Her soulless eyes lock onto mine. "And?"

All right. Clearly she feels five seconds is enough consideration. "Unfortunately, I guess I'm more like my mother's side of the family." I attempt a lighthearted chuckle.

Leticia nods once, and within seconds one of her goons has a hold of my shoulders and the other takes my crutches.

I know the situation is far from funny, but somehow the schoolyard bully tactic of taking my crutches just tickles my morose funny bone. I can't hide my grin.

"If you think Leticia Whitecloud is a woman with a sense of humor, Ms. Moon, you are sadly mistaken. Requests are only made once, and those who fail Leticia Whitecloud—don't require a second chance."

The tingling on the back of my neck and the burning of my mood ring confirm the twisty nausea in my gut. If I don't accept her job offer, it sounds as though I will not make it off this island alive. I suddenly recall how all the adventures on *Fantasy Island* took a dark turn.

She clenches her jaw.

The goon's hands tighten on my shoulders.

I toy with the idea of "hopping" for it, but it

seems my goose is well and truly plucked.

The door behind me smashes open, and for the first time during my visit to the casino, I see fear flash through Leticia Whitecloud's eyes.

"Step away from Miss Moon."

I don't need to turn around to imagine how powerfully intimidating Erick must look right now.

"You have no jurisdiction here, Sheriff." Leticia Whitecloud stands behind her desk and I see the bulge of a gun in her waistband.

"I have all the jurisdiction I need when involved in an active pursuit, Leticia." I sense Erick's uneasiness just below the surface of his swagger. "Hand her the crutches, Jimmy," he commands.

The one called "Jimmy" steps forward and puts the crutches out as I stand.

I take them and nod my thanks.

"Don't do anything stupid, Leticia. You may reign supreme on Hawk Island, but kidnapping one of my townsfolk is the quickest route to toppling your whole empire. So keep your hands where I can see them. That goes for your security, too."

As I crutch toward my rescuer, my heart races and uncontrolled sweat in my palms makes it difficult for my hands to grip the crutches. "Hello, Erick. I never pegged you for a gambler."

He keeps his gun trained on Ms. Whitecloud and gestures for me to walk past him.

Of course, this proves slightly more difficult with the shards from the broken door creating a bit of an obstacle course for the three-legged girl.

Erick whispers, “Please do not trip and fall right now.”

I focus all my attention on picking my way through the debris and making it out the door.

“See ya ’round.” Erick backs out of the office and protects my six as we slowly progress back through the skyway.

Once we’re on the other side of that door, he holsters his gun and says, “Hang on to your crutches, Moon.” He scoops me up and makes a hasty retreat out a side door toward his squad car in the parking lot.

“Silas is in my Jeep, over there.” I point to the vehicle.

Erick jogs over as the door pops open.

I’m not sure if Silas leaned across or if some otherworldly energy opened the door, but Erick slides me in, takes my crutches, and slams the door.

I’m about to open my window and protest as the back door opens and he tosses my crutches across the seat. “You two get outta here ASAP.”

He jogs back to his cruiser, and as soon as we’ve crossed the isthmus leading from the Hawk Island reservation back to Birch County proper, he hits the lights and whips past us toward Pin Cherry Harbor.

CHAPTER 17

I THINK it's safe to say I'm not a casino girl. I glance down at the untouched cup of hot chocolate in the cup holder and breathe a sigh of relief. "So, had you already called Erick when they brought you the cocoa?"

Silas nods. "I observed a well-dressed man exiting the front of the casino. Once he locked onto the Jeep and began to approach, I placed the call. Dispatch indicated it would be some time before a deputy could respond."

"Makes sense. It's at least a thirty-minute drive from Pin Cherry Harbor. How do you explain Erick getting on the scene so quickly?"

Silas shrugs his stooped shoulders. "I realize you manage to stay ahead of our fine sheriff, largely due to your gifts. However, you would be mistaken in underestimating his investigatory capacity. I have a strong suspicion that when you mentioned 'who had the most to lose' if your father's restorative justice organization went forward, Sheriff Harper placed Leticia Whitecloud very near the top of his list."

"When he smashed the door down—"

Silas lets out a low whistle. "My, my, that young man has it bad."

"What do you mean?"

"He technically has no jurisdiction on the reservation, Mitzy. Even the charismatic Sheriff Erick Harper is going to have his work cut out for him repairing that faux pas."

I think Silas might have missed the point of my question. I really don't give two hoots about jurisdiction. I was far more interested in what it is that the "young man" might have so badly. "Why do you think he took the risk?"

I watch as my lawyer's jowls shake with silent laughter. "Fishing for a compliment, are we?"

"Rude."

As we toddle down Main Street—Silas really is the world's slowest driver—I notice a cruiser parked in front of the bookshop. "Looks like I could be in a little bit of trouble, Silas. I may need you to accompany me inside, in a legal capacity."

"I know just what to do." Silas drives down the

freshly plowed alley and parks in the garage. We make our way in through the alley door and stop as we hear Twiggy and Erick in a heated argument.

"I'm telling you to mind your own business, Twiggy."

"Simmer down, Sheriff. You and I both know that he only has your best interest at heart. And I'll remind you, before you take that tone with me again, I used to change your diapers."

I'm powerless to contain the laughter that spills out of my mouth.

Erick spins toward me, his expression an odd combination of anger and embarrassment. "Miss Moon, I hate to be the one to point out how absolutely foolish it was for you to take on Leticia Whitecloud by yourself, and with a broken leg."

I angrily shamble toward Erick. "I'll have you know, I didn't 'take on' Leticia Whitecloud. I went out to the casino to redeem my voucher and a couple of her goons—actually three of her goons—escorted me into her office."

Erick crosses his arms in that delicious way that I find so distracting.

I can't help but smile.

"It's no joke, Mitzy. She's a dangerous woman."

"Mitzy Moon gathered that."

Erick scrunches up his face for a second, and then I see the lights go on as he recognizes my humorous use of the third person. He laughs in spite of the fact that he's not finished lecturing me. "And what was this voucher for?"

I swallow loudly and my eyes dart from Twiggy to Silas.

Twiggy for the win. Not so much that she rescues me; she throws me under the bus. "I'm sure you're familiar with the folly of youth, Sheriff. Her Royal Highness here is a little loose with her money. Probably gets it from her grandmother."

And as if on cue, I see Grams rocket down from the tin-plated ceiling shaking her finger at Twiggy.

"The nerve of her. She's the one who used to drive me out there all the time to help her cheat at poker. Unbelievable. I thought the rule was never to speak ill of the dead."

I'm in the middle of chuckling at Grams' snarky response when Erick says my name for what sounds like the second time—at least.

"Miss Moon, are you in there?"

"Sorry, I guess my throbbing ankle is distracting me."

"Why don't we continue this in the back room so you can sit down and elevate that leg." Erick leads the way and sets up two chairs.

I sit down, lay my crutches on the floor, and prop my foot on the second chair.

"So what's your game?"

If Erick thinks I'm going to share my scheme to uncover information about Judge Carlson's gambling habits, he's got another think coming. Fortunately, Silas comes to my actual rescue.

"She seems to be a fan of the roulette wheel."

"High risk. Little chance of reward. That sounds right." Erick shakes his head. "Well, my rescue efforts today will not be overlooked by the Tribal Council. If you made some kind of deal with the devil out there, you put me in a heckuva spot, Moon."

"I was just trying to redeem my voucher. She's the one who was pushing for a deal. I don't care how much birch vodka she makes me drink, I'm never going to say 'yes.'"

Erick uncrosses his arms, and once again I see his right hand brush the pocket of his coat. A strange energy washes over him and quickly vanishes. "What kind of offer did you refuse?"

"She was just fishing. I told her it was beginner's luck, and she seemed to think I might've had a system. She wanted to use me to sniff out cheaters."

"Talk about a fox in the hen house," Erick mumbles.

I leaned forward. "I'm sorry, what was that?"

"I'm just saying, I'm not sure who would regret that deal more."

Grams has a lovely belly laugh at my expense.

"I gotta head out early, doll. Have to make a couple of stops." Twiggy gives me a conspiratorial nod and wink. "I'll give you a full report tomorrow."

Silas shuffles across the floor and places a fatherly hand on my shoulder. "I think Mitzy could use some rest. Am I correct in assuming you will not be charging her with anything, Sheriff?"

Erick shakes his head. "Yes, sir. It would appear the Teflon queen has once again escaped justice."

He turns to leave.

"Erick, I'm sure you know Judge Carlson had a gambling problem."

He turns and fixes me with that impressed but exasperated stare. "And?"

"And if Leticia Whitecloud is willing to use force to convince winners to do her favors, what exactly do you think she would do to losers?"

Twiggy calls from the back door, "Don't forget to set the alarm, doll."

"Goodnight, Twiggy." I shrug and wait for Erick to react.

Nothing overt.

I give him credit for controlling his expression. My developing extra senses pick up on an electric shift in the sheriff's energy. He wasn't headed out to the Hawk Island Casino to rescue me; he already suspected.

CHAPTER 18

Twiggy shows up bright and early the next morning with information and doughnuts. Despite my aversion to early rising, those feelings do not extend to delicious doughnuts.

"So you went to the records office last night?"

"I had a little dinner and conversation."

I take a large chocolate éclair and relish each bite as Twiggy lays out the findings on the underground tunnels.

"So there are only two ways out?"

"That's right. One of them is an original entrance/exit in the basement of the building across the street. But that building was converted into a preschool three years ago and the owners live upstairs. Not exactly an ideal entry point for draggin' a dead body unnoticed."

"And the other one?" I cross my fingers.

"The other one comes from the abandoned service station on the corner of Birch and First Avenue."

"Have they checked that location?"

Twiggy nods. "They found signs of forced entry, but no prints."

I exhale and shake my head. "That doesn't surprise me. It's freezing cold. I'm sure they wore gloves the entire time."

"That's as good a theory as any."

"So now what?"

"They're following leads, but what you were saying to Sheriff Harper about losers got me thinking."

I hesitate to ask a follow-up question because I feel like I'm being set up. "Care to share?"

"What if Judge Carlson was on a big losing streak?"

The hairs on the back of my neck tingle and I know we're on to something. "So, what could he do for Leticia?"

"Maybe he did her legal favors?"

"Legal favors for the guys on her payroll?"

Twiggy nods. "I'm sure the guys on her payroll break the law more than every once in a while."

An eerie chill settles over me and my voice catches in my throat.

Grams fires into the room, giving voice to the thoughts still forming in my own head. "That's why she set up Jacob!"

Twiggy shivers. "Is it Isadora?"

"She's here. And I think she gave us our best lead so far. If Leticia Whitecloud was pressuring Judge Carlson to give her guys lighter sentences or probation to keep them indebted to her, then it stands to reason she would have the most to lose if my father started finding legitimate employment opportunities for ex-convicts. That gives her motive to frame my dad."

"Should we tell the sheriff?"

"Not yet. I still don't have a motive for the murder. If Judge Carlson was doing her favors, it hardly makes sense that she would take him out."

Grams swirls through. "Maybe he stopped cooperating after his wife passed away."

"No one reported him missing," I mumble, more to myself than anyone else.

Twiggy narrows her gaze. "What do you mean?"

"Well, some neighbor reported newspapers piling up on his front porch, but if he lived alone that would explain why no one reported him missing. Do you know when his wife passed away?"

Twiggy paces and mumbles, counting out something on her fingers.

"She passed away a few months before me." Grams sinks slowly toward the floor and shakes her head. "Losing a loved one changes you. I remember when my second husband died. I changed everything about my life. That's when I started going by Isadora—and finally sobered up. Some take a darker road."

"Do you think he started gambling more after his wife died?"

Before Grams has a chance to reply, Twiggy answers. "Maybe he felt like he didn't have anything to live for."

The strangely emotional observation from Twiggy makes me a little uncomfortable. "So his wife passes away, he loses himself in gambling, and possibly gets deeply in debt to the casino? If you were Leticia Whitecloud and you had something on a powerful judge who owes you a lot of money, why on earth would you kill him?"

A long silence hangs in our midst before Grams snaps it with a wild card from left field.

"Did Deputy Paulsen ever give you any information regarding the DNA Pyewacket collected from the break-in?"

I shift in my chair and tilt my head. "No. I'll call Erick right now." Pressing the speed dial for the non-emergency number to the station, I wait for an answer. "Sheriff Harper, please. Yes, it's Mitzy

Moon. I'm sure he is busy— I will hold." I gesture to the cast on my left leg. "If it wasn't for this dumb cast, I'd just walked down there. I can probably still get there faster on crutches than— Oh, hello, Erick."

Twiggy and Grams enjoy a chuckle at my expense.

"I meant to ask if you had any results on that DNA sample from the break-in? What? No, not the blood on the trophy. There was a hair sample. Maybe it even had a bit of scalp . . . Deputy Paulsen bagged it— Let me know what you find out. Oh, Erick, one more thing. Is there any way to find out if Judge Carlson had a significant gambling debt at the Hawk Island Casino?"

Grams floats in close to the phone, eagerly listening for the reply.

"I'm sure you are following all leads. If Deputy Paulsen is looking through old cases trying to find someone who was seeking revenge, I think she's barking up the wrong tree. Maybe she should be looking at the sentences for anyone associated with Leticia Whitecloud's operation— What I mean is, checking for any correlation between the judge's increasing gambling debt and bad guys getting lesser sentences . . . Thanks. Bye."

Twiggy walks toward the table. "What did he say?"

"He said he's not at liberty to discuss an on-going investigation."

Grams floats beside me. "Did you get any messages? Feelings? Images?"

"Nope. Maybe my psychic powers are on the fritz. I probably need some sleep."

But before I can make my way upstairs, the door to the alleyway opens and my dad walks in, his face a mask of concern.

"Hey, Dad, what's going on?"

"I keep thinking about Leroy Smith."

"He's the guy that you said served time for arson but claimed he was innocent, right?"

"Yeah, he said his wife set him up. He claimed it was some kind of revenge or punishment. Sounded pretty far-fetched at the time, but Odell just let me in on a piece of very interesting gossip."

Twiggy steps toward Jacob. "Well, are you gonna tell us? Or are you gonna make us beg?"

My dad grins. "Odell claims that Leroy Smith used to be married to Leticia Whitecloud."

I lean forward and use the table to help steady me on my feet. "Did Odell happen to mention if they had a child? Is she Victor's mother?

"Odell was pretty sure they had a kid. He didn't remember the name, though. But it all adds up. Leroy always said his old lady set him up so she could get custody. Based on your recent experience with Ms. Whitecloud, I'd say that sounds exactly like something she'd do."

I think back to how kind and friendly Victor was when he made his delivery. However, he didn't say anything about the burned building. Not even a passing comment. Is that odd or just polite? I have a hard time imagining he's related to the woman who was about to have her minions rough up a girl in a cast. "He kept his dad's name though?"

"When I was jumping through one of the many hoops created by the Historical Society, I shuffled past a lot of documents related to parcels of land owned by the Smith family. It's a pretty common name, but it stands to reason if it benefited her somehow then Leticia would've let Victor keep the name. Maybe there's some tie-in to her position with the tribal council." Jacob shrugs.

"Maybe. What we need to figure out is which of the pending cases on the list would've been important enough for Leticia to kill the judge."

My dad paces across the kitchen and shakes his head. "That's the part that doesn't make sense. If you have a federal judge in your pocket, you wouldn't kill him."

I glance at the ring on my left hand and receive no assistance. "We're missing something, Dad. We're definitely missing something."

"Well, I've got a meeting with Amaryllis. She's

trying to get the injunction set aside now that most of the building is destroyed, and move forward with a compromise that the Historical Society will accept. There's no telling if the new judge who'll be assigned to our case will be any better or worse for us than Judge Carlson." My father laughs coldly. "Although, it's hard to imagine it could be worse."

"Dad! You have to stop saying things like that."

He shakes his head. "Once a convict, always a suspect. You're right, Mitzy. I need to be more careful."

I feel guilty for making him uncomfortable. I want him to feel like he can be himself around me, but I can't help worrying that he might let something like that slip in front of the wrong person. "Would you mind dropping me off at the sheriff's station on your way to your meeting?"

"Is that cast on your leg interfering with your *interfering*?" He laughs a little too loudly.

But he's not wrong. "Actually, I think Erick's taking a little pity on me since the injury. I might be able to squeeze some information out of him just because I look so helpless."

"Talk about looks being deceiving." Jacob smiles and pats me on the shoulder. "Sit tight. I'll run upstairs and grab your cold weather gear. You okay to walk back?"

"Sure. I have this new thing where I just crutch

my way down the middle of the street until a car comes. Then I don't have to deal with the poorly shoveled sidewalk."

"Great." He rolls his eyes heavenward. "I'll be right back."

Technically, things could be worse. At least we have other possible suspects and we've located a solid point of entry for the tunnels. Hopefully, Erick will be in a sharing mood.

Jacob invites me to dinner and promises to introduce me to Amaryllis, while I promise to be on my best behavior. "Bye, dad."

Unfortunately for me, Deputy Paulsen is on her way out as I enter the station.

"Seems like you mighta bit off more than you can chew, taking on Leticia Whitecloud." One hand rests on the grip of her gun and the other wags a finger in my direction.

"I'm guessing that's a problem you've never had." I hobble through the swinging gate and make a beeline to Erick's office before she realizes how backhanded my compliment actually is.

He looks up and smiles as I walk in. "How's the ankle healing up?"

"It's definitely hurt my jump-shot game, but other than that I seem to be getting by."

He chuckles and gestures to the chair opposite his desk.

I get myself situated and lean my crutches across the chair next to me. "Any luck on that suspect list?"

"I've definitely moved Leticia Whitecloud to the top of the list."

"Who owns that abandoned gas station on Birch Street and First Avenue?"

Erick's eyes widen. "Looks like you're still handling left field all right." He tilts his head in an adorably obstinate way. "What's your interest?"

"If it's an access point to the tunnels, it stands to reason there could be a connection, right?"

"And who told you it was an entry to the tunnels?"

"I hear things. You don't fall through the floor of a burned out building, into a long-forgotten labyrinth of prohibition tunnels without some information trickling your way."

Erick leans back in his chair and laces his fingers behind his head. He smiles at me, and for a second one of my gifts picks up a hint of disappointment.

Normally I wouldn't have been able to keep my eyes from peering toward the potential of washboard abs, but somehow I manage to control myself. That's real progress, for those of you keeping score at home. I grin and lean forward. "Who owns the building, Erick?"

"That piece of property belongs to the Hawk Island Land Trust."

"Any connection to the Hawk Island Casino?"

"Officially, the land trust was formed by the tribal council to use gambling related profits to buy back tribal lands."

I tilt my head and smile. "And unofficially?"

Erick leans forward and I can smell the clean citrus-woodsy notes of his skin and see that hint of touchable stubble on his chin.

"Unofficially, the Hawk Island Land Trust is nothing more than a front for Leticia Whitecloud's money laundering."

"Who owned the property before the land trust?"

"The old service station was originally built by Leroy Smith's great-grandfather."

"The convicted arsonist?" I lean back and raise an eyebrow. "That's interesting."

"Just between us, I'm beginning to think you're right about Leticia Whitecloud framing your dad."

You could knock me over with a feather. Unless my ears deceive me, or my gift of clairaudience somehow garbled the message, I honestly think Erick Harper just agreed with me—and it's just between us. We're in cahoots! I take a deep breath and struggle to steady my voice. "Are you saying you believe my father is innocent?"

Erick shuffles some papers on his desk and takes a sip of—what has to be the world's coldest—coffee before he answers. "You and I both know your dad isn't an *innocent*. But I'm pretty sure he didn't have anything to do with what happened to Judge Carlson. We checked into that eyewitness, and she had more than one inexplicable deposit in her bank account."

I want to jump up and down and pound my fist on Erick's desk as I shout, "I told you so! I told you so!" But I'm going to stop sabotaging my own chances with this gorgeous man, and try to be a gracious winner. "I appreciate that you followed up on my hunch."

His face pales and his jaw clenches. His eyes focus on a point faraway. "I wish I had listened to you before the incident at the casino. If I hadn't already been on my way out there . . . Like I told you before, you're lucky. Not everyone's that lucky." His voice goes so soft. I barely hear his last few words. And he's still not looking at anything in this room.

I don't know what happened in Afghanistan, but maybe one day he'll trust me enough to tell me. Today I'm just going to celebrate the fact that my dad is no longer a suspect, and get back to work connecting the dots between Leticia Whitecloud and Judge Carlson. "Hey, I heard Paulsen was looking into Judge Carlson's old cases. What about those pending cases on his docket? If Leticia Whitecloud framed my dad, maybe the reason she framed him and the reason she killed Judge Carlson are connected."

Erick nods and his focus slowly returns to the sheriff's station. "I'm looking into that. She's definitely got ex-cons on her payroll and it seems like Judge Carlson's gambling habit spun out of control after his wife died last year. We're still going through bank records and case files. I have to get all my ducks in a row before I go after someone like Leticia Whitecloud."

"Copy that. Let me know if there's anything I can do."

He laughs a little under his breath as he stands. "I'd tell you to stay out of this, mind your own business, and keep your head down, but I'm starting to figure out that's not how you operate."

"I don't go looking for trouble . . ."

"Yet, somehow it always seems to find you." He stands as he shakes his head.

I get my crutches adjusted and tripod my way out of the station. Hesitating at the front door, I turn, hoping to catch a glimpse of Erick returning to his office, but instead I discover that he's watching me walk away with a very suspicious grin on his face.

Our eyes meet, and he runs a nervous hand

through his hair, loosening a few slicked-back strands of those sexy blond bangs before he retreats to the safety of his office.

I take a deep breath and push out the front door into the welcome rush of cold air.

CHAPTER 19

THE SUN IS SETTING and the temperature has definitely dropped outside. But as I crutch my way down Main Street, the bliss of my perfect meeting with Erick is warming me from the inside out. I hear a vehicle approaching and I scoot over to the side of the road.

To my surprise it's not a car this time, but a snowmobile. I'm still smiling like a lunatic when the snowmobile comes to a stop beside me.

The driver wears a full-face helmet, which looks very similar to a motorcycle helmet.

Smiling, I give friendly wave.

The driver doesn't remove his helmet. Instead, he jumps off the snowmobile, knocks my crutches to the ground, and forces me onto the sled.

I scream, but his leather-mittened hand clamps over my mouth.

I struggle, but I've got a broken leg, and the guy outweighs me by at least a hundred pounds. My efforts are utterly in vain.

I bite his hand, as hard as I can, but, recalling how handy my thick leather gloves were in protecting me against Pyewacket's claws, I'm sure my assailant feels nothing.

The snowmobile roars to life and he rips down Main Street straight toward the dead end overlooking the massive frozen lake. He shows no sign of stopping and I scream with renewed terror as we launch off the snowbank, down the escarpment, and onto the frozen lake.

Driving vehicles on lakes is not a thing we do in Arizona. I have never crossed a frozen lake in my life, and I know next to nothing about the buoyancy of snowmobiles.

Once we travel away from the glow cast by the streetlights of Pin Cherry Harbor, my captor puts both hands to work steering the snowmobile and increases his speed from fear-inducing to ludicrous.

Leave it to my strange little brain to find a humorous *Spaceballs* reference in the midst my kidnapping.

We travel along the frozen great lake, staying near land, and then briefly cross a road, blast through a field, and finally the headlights illuminate a much smaller lake. Maybe it's not a lake. It's perfectly flat, and there are no trees, but there are a few very tiny houses.

My cheeks and ears burn with cold, and a tear is frozen in the corner of my right eye.

My captor parks behind one of the miniature buildings, turns off the snowmobile, and roughly drags me inside the structure.

I'm doing the best I can to protect my ankle, but I really shouldn't be putting any weight on it.

He pushes me onto a small camping chair in the corner of a five-foot-by-six-foot space. Winds buffet the walls and whistle through unseen cracks. He crouches and lights a match. A short while later, I see flames roaring inside a tiny furnace.

He takes off his helmet, and for the first time I see the face of my kidnapper.

"Victor?"

"Sorry about this, Miss Moon."

"What are you doing? Why did you bring me here?"

"I can't tell you anything. We just gotta stay here until I get the call. Then I'll take you back. Nobody gets hurt."

I sit perfectly still and realize that my phone is still in the pocket of my jacket. Sooner or later he's going to have to go outside to relieve himself. That should give me just enough time to call Erick. Holy crap, I hope my battery is charged! Time to let junior know he's not dealing with an amateur. "Look, Victor, I don't know what your mom's promising you, but there's a better way out of this than holding me for ransom."

The firelight flickers across his face, and I see a flash of concern while my extrasensory perception picks up on some nervousness tinged with guilt. "It's really better if you stay quiet," he whispers through gritted teeth.

"Victor, what does your mom have on you? Is she threatening to send your dad to prison again?"

He stands up and lunges for me.

I lean back and scream.

He sits down and punches one fist into the palm of the other hand and runs both hands through his hair several times. "I told you to be quiet. You have to be quiet. My mom said you'd be quiet."

All right. Note to self: Victor seems mildly imbalanced. Maybe talking about his Mafia mother and his arsonist father isn't the best approach.

"I'm sorry, Victor. I didn't mean to upset you. I won't say anything more about your parents. But I can't be quiet. It's not in my nature. Maybe you can tell me all about your snowmobile?"

The energy in the room takes a distinctive shift

toward calm. Emotional time-bomb temporarily defused.

"Tell me about your sled."

Victor launches into an extremely technical presentation of the pros and cons of various types of sleds, and alloy skis versus compression-molded skis versus rubber track versus four-stroke. I'm just making things up now. I lost interest at least ten minutes ago. I honestly don't care what he says, as long as he keeps talking.

I nod and give appreciative monosyllabic exclamations where appropriate.

Eventually, the topic loses steam and Victor gets to his feet.

I hold my breath, hoping this might be the moment he goes outside.

Instead, he leans over and takes a long wooden pole from a clasp on the wall. As it passes in front of the fire, I see very sharp, very shiny metal points on the end. It looks like the Devil's pitchfork—only with more spikes.

I gasp. "Victor, please don't hurt me."

"What?" He looks down and laughs.

The laughter makes my skin crawl.

"This? This is a fishing spear. I am going to catch dinner." He leans down, grabs a leather strap, and pulls a chunk of the floor straight up. Then he takes his spear and breaks through a thin layer of ice, exposing a two-foot-by-three-foot square of ridiculously cold slush water.

Now I'm not only afraid of being stabbed, but I'm also afraid I may be drowned in frigid water.

He tosses something into the water and places the tip of the spear in the surface. He leans toward the hole and holds perfectly still. His eyes seem to bore into the depths of the lake.

I lean forward a little, but I don't see anything. I lose track of how much time passes.

Victor does not move.

And suddenly, like a rattlesnake striking its prey, he launches the spear into the depths. A strap around his wrist snaps tight and he pulls the spear back up to reveal a very large, very bloodied fish, skewered on several of the tines.

My stomach roils and I turn away.

He holds the spear in one hand and reaches into a cooler with the other. He hands me a bottle of water and smiles like a friendly host. "I'll go clean this and be right back. Here's some water in case you're thirsty."

I take the bottle and nod. "Thank you."

He opens the door of this little building and I hold my breath, hoping that he's going to close it. He maneuvers the spear and the fish through the opening, steps out, and closes the door.

I have no idea how long it takes to clean a fish,

but I'm guessing it's not his first time so it probably won't take that long. I reach into my coat pocket, check to make sure the ringer is on "silent" and dial. I don't dare lift the phone to my ear. I'd never be able to get it back inside my pocket if the door opened. I strain with every fiber of my being and I can barely hear ringing.

The ringing stops.

I'm sure I can hear a voice.

I can't take the risk that Victor will come back in and hear that same voice. I turn the volume down until there's no sound and I slip the phone back into my pocket. Hopefully, the signal can be tracked.

All I can do now is hope that Erick is as smart as I think he is.

The door opens and Victor comes back in carrying two large fillets. "Ever had northern pike?"

"No, I haven't."

He takes a small cast-iron skillet off a hook on the wall and sets it on top of the little potbellied stove.

I have to admit that a degree of relief washes over me when I see him put the fillets in the frying pan. I was beginning to worry my first taste of northern pike was going to be raw.

Victor returns his spear to the clamp and places the board back over his fishing hole. He sits down on a camping chair opposite me and monitors the cooking fish. A few minutes pass and I keep wondering if the battery in my phone lasted long enough for Erick to figure out why I was calling and trace the call, or triangulate the cell signal, or some other locating magic.

Victor grabs a plate and scrapes one of the fillets out of the pan. He drops it on the plate and hands it to me. "No forks, sorry."

"That's all right. I'll use my fingers. It won't be the first time."

He smiles warmly, like we're old friends, and shoves a handful of fish in his mouth.

I tentatively tear off a small chunk and give it a taste.

"Watch out for bones." He mumbles through his mouthful of fish.

And yet another way for me to die. Choking to death on a fishbone.

If my battery had some juice and my phone is still on and there's any chance Erick can hear me, I should probably start dropping some clues. "So Victor, what is this place?"

"You never been in a fish house?"

"Oh, this is an ice-fishing house. Is it your ice-fishing house?" Jiminy Cricket, I'm talking too loud. He doesn't seem to notice.

Victor chews on some more fish and nods.

"Yeah, me and my dad come out here. He taught me how to fish."

"Wow, that's neat. Maybe I can get my dad to teach me how to ice fish."

He shakes his head. Carefully works the fish around in his mouth and picks three bones out before he comments. "I don't think your dad will be around."

My chest tightens uncomfortably and I feel like I can't take a breath. "He's not moving away. He's just selling the house out by the lake."

"No. Never mind."

"What do you mean, Victor? You can tell me what's going on. It's just me and you." I point to my leg. "It's not like I'm going anywhere." I try to chuckle lightheartedly.

"Yeah, sorry about that. I didn't know about the leg until I saw you on the road. I almost wasn't going to do it but—"

"Your mom's kinda tough to refuse."

He clenches his jaw tightly and I can see he's fighting down a bit of anger, but this time he doesn't lose his temper. "Yeah, pretty much."

"So what did you mean about my dad?"

"That's why she had me take you."

"I thought you said this wasn't for ransom?"

"No, she needs your dad to do something."

The hair on the back of my neck tingles. My mood ring turns to ice on my left hand. Everything is deadly clear. No, this isn't for ransom. Leticia Whitecloud is going to force my dad to confess to Judge Carlson's murder. She knows he would do anything for me. Time for me to start spreading some dis-information.

"I hate to break it to you, Victor. But my dad and I just met. There's no way he's going to throw away his life and go back to prison for me."

Victor goes completely still. His large brown eyes glisten in the firelight. "You'd be surprised what parents would do for their children."

For a moment it feels like time is standing still. My heart's not beating. My lungs refuse to take in a breath. My mind is utterly frozen.

Victor Smith killed Judge Carlson.

CHAPTER 20

Now that the murderous cat is out of the bag, I have far more questions than answers. Why on earth would Victor kill the judge? When did Victor kill the judge? Did this kind young man who delivered my Valentine surprise from Rory actually bash in a man's skull?

Nothing is adding up. And to make matters worse, my genius, television-inspired, cell-phone-tracking plan seems like it's—

Victor jumps to his feet and I gasp in fear.

He shushes me and seems to be listening to—

Now I hear it too. There's a snowmobile approaching.

He leans toward me and whispers, "Just keep quiet. That's probably somebody headed out to their ice house."

On the outside I appear calm. But on the inside my heart is pounding like a drum and my mind is whirring.

The snowmachine is definitely getting closer.

Victor is agitated and, based on my latest psychic revelation, I'm genuinely afraid of what he might do. The sound is getting louder and the machine is probably right outside the little house.

The engine shuts off.

Victor is absolutely still.

"Victor Smith, this is Sheriff Harper. Come out of the ice house with your hands up."

Victor grabs the knife he used to clean the fish with one hand, yanks me out of my camping chair, and tucks me under his other arm like a ragdoll.

"No one needs to get hurt, Victor. I only want to talk to you. Just come out with your hands up and we'll have a little chat."

With my head pressed against his winter coat, I can hear Victor's heart beating through his chest and all of my senses pick up on his fear and panic.

"I'm coming out," Victor shouts.

I note that he makes no mention of dragging out a hostage at knifepoint.

The door opens and the sheriff stands outside, illuminated by the snowmobile's headlight. His gun is trained on Victor. It only takes a second for him to spot me—and the knife in Victor's other hand.

"Let her go, Victor. This is between you and me. We're just gonna have a little chat. No one needs to get hurt."

"I don't want to hurt anyone, Sheriff. I never wanted to hurt anyone. Just let me get on my sled."

"You know I can't let you do that, Victor. Mitzy doesn't have anything to do with this. Let her go and then I can help you."

"I can't let her go. My mom wants her."

A movement in the shadows startles Victor and he moves the knife to my throat.

My father's tense voice cuts the crisp night air. "Victor, it's Jake Duncan. I'm the one your mom really wants. You let Mitzy go and you can take me straight to your mom. No questions asked. I'll cooperate. Just let Mitzy go."

His voice cracks when he says my name and it breaks my heart.

"I can't do that, man." Victor drags me roughly toward his sled. Keeping my body between him and Erick's gun.

My dad takes a step toward us, and Victor wields the knife. "Stay back. I don't want to hurt her, but I will."

"Duncan, get back on the sled. You're not helping." Erick's voice is strained. But the next sentence he utters is colder than the wind swirling through the frozen darkness. "If you run, Victor, this will not end well for you."

Victor shoves me onto the snowmobile, climbs on behind me, and fires up the engine. A second later we're racing across the frozen lake. He has to drop the knife and grab both handlebars to control the sled at this speed.

The fact that there's no blade at my throat doesn't make this ride any less terrifying. There's barely a sliver of moon hanging in the sky and the headlight illuminates precious little. I can almost imagine my life ending with the sled impacting a tree.

There's another vehicle in pursuit. A lone headlight bobbing and weaving in the silvery blackness.

That's when I remember a little piece of trivia. Victor Smith is the six-time Iron Sled Race champion. It seems frighteningly unlikely that Erick, despite his many skills, will be able to catch this award-winning sledder.

Icy wind knifes through us as Victor pushes his snowmobile to its limit. We make a sharp left and seem to be following a small frozen creek. The narrow trail between the trees suddenly opens into another vast expanse of frozen lake, or possibly field. Victor leans forward as he tries to force the throttle to open farther.

Unbelievably, the other snowmachine is gaining on us.

In the movies there would be wild gunfire. Perhaps the pursuing vehicle would shoot out our tread and send our snowmobile into an end-over-end roll, resulting in neither Victor nor me being injured, but I'd be thrown free of my captor.

There are no gunshots. No miraculous accident that ends my kidnapping. Instead, the pursuing vehicle slowly gains on us and I can feel Victor's panic growing.

Before I know it, the other snowmobile is directly beside us.

There's only one person on the sled—my dad.

Victor leans into a turn and our snowmachine tilts dangerously.

My father matches Victor's every move and things happen so fast I'm not sure if I'm having a premonition, a vision, or simply witnessing the unbelievable events as they occur.

Victor attempts to swerve into my dad.

Jacob somehow avoids the collision but leaps onto our sled, dragging Victor and me into the deep snow as the sleds fly off in the other direction and collide.

I expected more pain. The deep snow is surprisingly forgiving.

My father twists Victor's arms behind him and

somehow secures his wrists with a belt in two seconds flat. "Go get the sled, Mitzy."

Regardless of the doctor's instructions, without crutches, in deep snow, I'm going to have to put a little weight on my ankle. I hobble-hop over to the sled. It's still upright and somehow running. I try to mimic Victor's actions.

The snowmobile jerks forward and I fall back, but manage to hang on to the handlebars. I putter around and come back toward my dad.

He looks at me and his adrenaline-dilated pupils are almost glowing in the faint moonlight.

"You drive back and get Sheriff Harper. This guy's not going anywhere." He yanks Victor's bound wrists.

I would absolutely love to do what my father says, but I have no idea where we are and even less of an idea how to get back to Erick. "I don't actually know where we are."

My father takes a deep breath and I can sense a calmness settling over him. "Right." He yanks Victor to his feet. "Come on, kid. We're gonna get that other sled back on its skis." He tugs Victor toward the sled with one hand and with the other he shockingly manages to yank the snowmobile upright.

Despite the pain and cold, it warms my heart to think my dad might be a little bit of a superhero.

He pushes Victor onto the sled, climbs on behind, and his powerful arms encircle the man who threatened my life. Jacob motors toward me and calls, "Follow me."

"Copy that," I say with far more confidence than I feel. Driving a snowmobile twenty or thirty feet at low speed is one thing, following my father through the dark of night, in completely unknown surroundings, will be another story altogether.

About halfway back, we see the headlight of another sled approaching. The headlamp flashes off and on—twice.

My father seems to know the signal and flashes his own headlight.

Within seconds the sled circles around and Sheriff Erick pulls up next to me. "Stop your sled," he shouts.

I do as I'm told, but in spite of the frightful events of the evening, I'm laughing on the inside. This has got to be one of the most unusual traffic stops in history.

Erick abandons his vehicle, jumps on the back of mine, and takes control of the steering.

As his strong arms engulf me, a wave of relief-tears threatens to burst forth. I swallow hard, take several deep icy breaths, and blink as hard as I can. I will not cry. I will not cry.

With Erick following my dad, our speed increases greatly and within minutes we're racing past the ice-fishing house that I'm sure I will never forget.

When we reach the road, there are two cruisers waiting with lights flashing.

Erick jumps off our sled, grabs Victor, swaps my dad's belt for a set of actual handcuffs, and shoves Victor rather roughly into the back of one of the cruisers.

"Paulsen, get another deputy out here to take care of the sleds. Baird, get out to Smith's ice house and bag and tag everything."

I squint my eyes against the flashing red and blue lights and am shocked to learn that Furious Monkeys is Deputy Baird. Not only was I unaware that she ever left the front desk, but clearly I had no idea she had a name.

Paulsen approaches the sheriff. "You takin' him back to the station?" She juts a finger toward Victor.

"Nope. He can sit in the back of the cruiser until he rots."

Paulsen's eyes widen. "Things all right, Sheriff?"

I resist the urge to blurt out my unsubstantiated accusations against Victor Smith. But I'm pleased when I hear Erick say, "He killed Judge Carlson. We have to connect the dots for the prosecution, but I'm telling you right now, Deputy, he did it."

Paulsen caresses the handle of her gun as she replies, "We'll make it stick, Sheriff. We'll make it stick."

"Jacob, Mitzy, let me give you a ride back to town." Erick climbs in the driver's side of the second cruiser and my father opens the front door to let me in the passenger side.

I shake my head and open the rear passenger door. "You sit in front, Dad. You sit in front." I'm pretty proud that I didn't cry when I said it, but as soon as I settle into the back of the patrol car, silent tears trickle down my cheeks.

A sudden thought bursts into my head, and you know how much trouble I have with patience. "Erick, why did you let my dad have the sled and chase down Victor?"

Erick chuckles. "*Let* your dad?" He shakes his head

"Dad?"

"Two things you need to know, Mitzy. First, I don't need permission to save your life. Second, Victor Smith isn't the only one who's got a stack of Iron Sled championship trophies."

As my father chuckles, I shake my head. I really don't know very much about this man.

"Seems like your family is just full of surprises." Erick smacks his hand on the steering wheel and enjoys a little chuckle at the Duncan/Moon expense.

The remainder of our ride back to town is peppered with my father's retelling of the chase and Erick's exclamations of praise and concern.

As the fear and adrenaline slowly drain away, the throbbing ache of my left ankle takes center stage.

CHAPTER 21

Erick drops me off at the hospital. He didn't ask or tell, he just did. He pulled straight into the emergency entrance and instructed the orderlies to put me on a gurney. "I'll send Silas to pick you up."

"Thanks. Any chance someone turned my crutches in to lost and found?"

Erick looks at the ground. "I found 'em."

So many questions race through my mind as the medical staff wheels me inside.

Turns out I'm a fast healer, and other than some swelling from too much activity, my ankle is all right. The doctor swaps out the cast for a Velcro boot/splint thingy and tells me to schedule a follow-up in two weeks.

My father schedules the appointment before I can protest.

Having lost all track of time, I'm shocked to discover the sun is up when we come out of the medical center and climb into my waiting Jeep, chauffeured by my attorney.

Silas was keeping Grams company during my absence and he reports that she is fit to be tied. With her improved abilities to interact with physical objects, she's been able to write short notes to him and they made it work.

He was instructed to bring us straight back to the bookshop, but after two solid minutes of my begging and pleading he breaks.

"I shall acquiesce to your entreaty." Silas shakes his head and his jowls jiggle.

After a sleepless night and extremely low blood sugar, I laugh far too easily and too long.

"I'm pleased my agreement amuses, Mitzy."

My dad reaches up from the back seat and pats my shoulder. "We need to get some food in this girl, stat."

We both giggle uncontrollably.

Silas harrumphs into his mustache. "Never let it be said that exercise and fresh air fail to lift the spirits."

Now I'm LOL-ing so hard that tears are leaking out of my eyes. "If by exercise you mean kidnapping, and by fresh air you mean the oily gas fumes of a snowmobile—then, yup."

My dad smacks his leg, guffaws, and struggles to catch his breath. "I gotta say, I'm sorta looking forward to staying indoors for a while."

Silas parks in front of the diner and my dad helps me out of the car.

As he hands over my recovered crutches, I get a horrible flashback to Victor grabbing me off the street and all the humor gets sucked right out of me.

Jacob circles an arm around my shoulders and kisses the top of my head. "It's over, sweetie. You're safe."

"Let us partake of the township's finest sustenance and put the events of last night in our rearview." Silas holds the door of Myrtle's Diner open as I crutch in—to a standing ovation.

Odell walks out from the kitchen clapping, slowly.

Tally and the two regulars at the counter join in the applause.

I blush and fake a curtsy. "Sit down. Stop it already. I really can't take any credit. All I did was get kidnapped. Sheriff Erick did all the real work."

The clapping abruptly stops and I'm a little disappointed. I planned to milk the adoration for a few more minutes and possibly fit in one or two more humble-brags—

"I really can't take all the credit either," says a familiar and sexy voice behind me.

"Erick?"

He nods and continues. "You all should've seen Jacob Duncan on that sled!"

Another round of applause brings a healthy ruddy glow to my father's cheeks.

Silas steps over and shakes Erick's hand. "Another fine job, sir. Would you care to join us for a celebratory meal?"

I clench my jaw and steal myself against the refusal.

"I'd like that. Thanks, Silas."

What just happened? Did I hit my head and wake up in Bizarro world?

My dad winks at me, leans my crutches in the corner, and helps me out of my coat.

I shudder to think what I actually look like after my harrowing night, but the urgent messages growling up from my stomach silence the protests of vanity.

Jacob leans down and whispers, "True, but maybe we can change that."

I scrunch up my face in confusion and shrug.

He points to my shirt and snorts a little when he laughs.

Embarrassingly, my shirt bears a list of three things, each preceded by a check box: SINGLE; TAKEN; HUNGRY—only "hungry" is checked.

We take one side of the booth, and Silas and Erick take the other.

"How is the case shaping up?" asks Silas.

Erick chuckles. "I expected Mitzy to ask that."

A round of laughter takes the table.

I lean forward. "But seriously, what's the deal?"

He nods. "Victor made a full confession and he's agreed to testify against Leticia Whitecloud."

I nod, patronizingly. "Great tagline for the movie poster, Erick, but we're gonna need some details. I'm having a real hard time believing that Victor acted alone."

Erick bobs his head up and down. "You would be correct. Victor was on an enforcing assignment for his mom. Judge Carlson was into the Hawk Island Casino for almost one hundred thousand. Leticia had him 'paying' his debt by commuting sentences and dismissing cases. He was supposed to give one of her top guys probation for assault with a deadly weapon, but he couldn't do it."

Silas tamps down his mustache with a thumb and finger. "Every man has his limits."

We all nod.

"Victor went to the judge's chambers to rough him up, but Carlson got angry and told Victor how Leticia set up Leroy. He told him Leroy never set that fire, back in the day. It was all part of Leticia's plan to get custody."

"Son of a gun, he was tellin' the truth." My dad leans back and shakes his head in disbelief.

"Right?" Erick shakes his head. "Well, Victor has a real temper. He shoved the judge and the old man slipped and fell right onto the corner of his desk. The kid panicked and ran to his mom."

A twinge of jealousy stabs into my heart. Not that I'd ever want to commit a terrible crime, but it must be nice to have a mother to run to—maybe not if that mother is Leticia Whitecloud.

"She came up with the whole plan. Framing Jacob. Getting one of her guys to 'create' and hide the murder weapon. She even knew about the old tunnels and sent Leroy and the other guy down to stash the body and set up the fire."

I slap my hand on the table. "I knew there were two guys."

Erick looks at me and leans back. He tilts his head and fixes me with a piercing stare. "You knew quite a few things. I'm a little concerned about the details you 'stumbled' upon, Miss Moon."

I chuckle as lightheartedly as I can. "Let's not ruin a perfect breakfast with formalities, Erick. You can call me Mitzy."

Erick goes on to explain how Leticia's empire will implode if Leroy and Victor turn state's evidence. Her illegal gambling operations at the bingo hall, Decameron Downs horse track, and all of her off-the-books, high-stakes poker games will be a thing of the past.

It's probably for the best if I don't mention the Scrabble. I might have used up all of my "get out of jail free cards."

Tally slides our delicious breakfasts onto the table and all conversation evaporates in the face of the mouth-watering meals.

I'm the first one to come up for air. Not that anyone will find that terribly shocking. "So, Victor accidentally killed Judge Carlson?"

"Correct."

"What's gonna happen to him?" Silas and my dad lay down their forks, wipe their mouths, and wait for Erick's reply.

"There were already several federal agencies involved in various investigations into Leticia's operations. So, Leroy and Victor will get a barely supervised walk in the park in exchange for their testimony."

"Will they have to enter witness protection?" Jacob asks.

"They asked to. Leroy said things were never the same after his stint in Clearwater. He doesn't want Victor to have to deal with all that."

My dad leans back and clears his throat. "It's not easy—the stigma. People don't forgive as quick as you'd like."

Erick takes a sip of his coffee, wipes his mouth, and sets his hands in his lap. "I misjudged you, Jacob. I tend to see the worst of people's choices in my line of work and it colors my opinions."

Jacob and Erick exchange head nods, and I feel like I just watched some alternate species exchange a powerful communication, but I clearly don't speak the language.

"I appreciate that." My dad finishes his coffee.

"Think nothing of it," says Erick.

I exhale and shrug. No matter how long I observe them, I'll never understand men. "I better get back to the bookshop. Grams—"

Jacob and Silas both "whip pan" to me like the scene in a movie where the record needle scratches across the vinyl.

I attempt to recover my horrible fumble. "Grams' friend Twiggy needed to go over some bookstore stuff with me." Most of the sentence is mumbled under my breath as I struggle to get out of the booth before I wedge my entire broken ankle in my mouth.

My dad hands my crutches to me and whispers as he hugs me, "Nice save, Gretzky."

I laugh, because regardless of my Arizona upbringing, I actually know that Wayne Gretzky was a hockey player. Now, don't ask me for what team or what position, or even when, but he definitely played hockey.

I give the guys a wave and my father drives me back to the Bell, Book & Candle. I offered to walk/crutch, but no one was having it.

Lucky me. I survived my abduction and returned to civilization just in time to make good on my bingo-related promises.

CHAPTER 22

My stomach is still a little unsettled from the drive over. Twiggy is a little *extra* behind the wheel. She handles a car like she's a New York City bike messenger that has to deliver a package before the stock exchange closes. My breakfast, lunch, and dinner all seem to be caught in a mini hurricane inside my stomach. However, the bracingly cold air outside the Elks Lodge is quite an effective remedy. By the time I "crutch" my way into the bingo hall, my head is clear and I'm breathing easier. Then I remember how I have to pretend to enjoy my evening with Wayne's friend. A man probably three times my age and possibly having very few of his original teeth. Regardless, I have no regrets. If I have to take one for the team, at least I was able to protect my dad's freedom and prove his innocence.

One night with Wayne's stodgy friend is a small price to pay.

Twiggy breezes past me and some man, who I'm assuming is Wayne, gives her a friendly hug.

The look on her face is a cross between happiness and embarrassment. It's quite a novel expression and I can't tear my eyes away. But before she can get too comfortable, Wayne comes over to introduce himself and pumps my arm wildly.

"Good to finally meet you, Mitzy."

Still pumping my arm.

"And you, Wayne."

Still.

"I sure do appreciate you keeping up your end of the deal—this time." He tosses me a sly grin and finally releases my dizzy arm.

I choose not to take the bait. "Not even a broken ankle could keep me away, Wayne."

He chuckles and slaps me on the back so hard I nearly lose my balance, despite my tripod.

I'm anxious to get this night over with. "Well, you should probably introduce me to your friend."

Wayne's sly grin widens and he gives me a little wink.

My stomach is back to nauseous flip-flopping.

"I think you might've already met." Wayne steps to the side and makes a grand gesture as his friend approaches. "Miss Moon, Erick Harper."

My eyes are still working their way up from the floor and they stop for far too long on the very well-fitted jeans. By the time they get all the way up to the stubbled chin, piercing blue eyes, and the lovely blond bangs hanging casually to the side, my heart skips a beat and my tummy tingles in a whole new way.

"Good evening, Miss Moon."

"Good evening, Erick."

"Well, now that we're all acquainted, let's play some bingo." Wayne slaps Erick on the back and walks up on stage.

Erick leans toward me and whispers, "Do you want me to get some cards for you? I saved us some seats over there." He points to the table at the front of the room. Former home to Pink Sweater, who will absolutely go down with Leticia's ship for her part in the scam. She and the previous caller had a system in place to make sure the house, or rather Leticia, always stayed ahead. Looks like her days of faking "bingos" are over. I smile with more wicked satisfaction than necessary. "Sure. I'll be waiting at the table."

He nods.

I crutch my way toward the table and Twiggy takes a seat next to me.

Wayne is up on stage making some general announcements and then he addresses the subject of the recent arrests. "And I just want everyone to know that the Elks Lodge has severed all ties with Leticia Whitecloud and the Hawk Island Casino. We're running our own bingo games free and clear. All proceeds go to support the local animal shelter and the winter heating-assistance program for veterans."

Uproarious cheers and thunderous applause fill the bingo hall.

"And just to make sure we get our fresh start off on the right foot. We have a special caller who is truly beyond reproach. Ladies and gents, please give a round of applause for tonight's caller, Sheriff Erick Harper!"

Chairs scrape back as everyone in the bingo hall gets to their feet and gives Erick a standing ovation. I self-consciously struggle with my crutches and do my best to get to my feet as well, clapping clumsily while attempting to squeeze a crutch under each arm.

Erick climbs the steps to the stage, and, humble as always, waves everyone to sit down immediately. "You're all too kind. Too kind indeed. I am pleased we will be able to bring Judge Carlson's killer to justice and shut down the gambling ring that was destroying far too many families here in Pin Cherry Harbor. But I would be remiss to take all the credit.

Several of my fine deputies went above and beyond on this one."

Thunderous applause, cheers, and I swear I hear someone chanting "Paulsen, Paulsen" in the back of the room. I scoff a little under my breath.

"And I'm sure most of you've heard about the important contributions of our own local hero, Mitzy Moon. Without her amazing clumsiness we may never have discovered the underground tunnels that allowed Judge Carlson's killers to hide their criminal activities."

I shake my head and cover my face in embarrassment.

A lot of laughter and a smattering of applause trickle throughout the hall.

"But, truth be told, Miss Moon provided several valuable leads on this case, and I for one am happy to have a concerned citizen like her living in our fair town. Miss Moon, will you join me on stage and check the calls?"

I shake my head and point to my ankle.

"Can somebody bring a chair up here for Miss Moon?"

Several industrious locals jump up, and before I know it two chairs have been placed on stage, and Wayne is dragging me up the stairs.

Despite his modesty, Erick has a natural charm that endears him to the audience. After the first couple of games, he starts to loosen up. By the time Tally wins her first bingo, he's feeling relaxed enough to pretend she's falsified her card and starts to read her rights.

The crowd goes wild and Tally blushes almost as red as her hair.

"We're only kiddin' around. She's got a bingo fair and square. Pay the lady." Erick nods to the cashier and Tally walks to the far end of the stage and collects her winnings.

Gone are the days of Hawk Island Casino vouchers and some shady lady skimming off the top.

I make an acceptable Vanna White and, after the last bingo is called, Erick offers to drive me home.

"Oh, thanks." My heart is flip-flopping and my tummy tingles. But right on the two-yard-line, I drop all my marbles—as Grams would say. "I better ride back with Twiggy. She drove my Jeep over and she doesn't . . . I shouldn't make her . . ." My lie generator is stuck. For the first time in my post-mom life, I can't make up a story.

He looks away and slips into his coat. "No worries. You ladies need to stick together." He smiles weakly and his hand brushes against the pocket of his jacket and hesitates.

For the third time, I wonder what the heck is in that pocket.

This time his hand slips in the pocket and pulls out a slightly tattered envelope. "I meant to give this to you on Val—before. But then you went and crashed through the floor of that burned out building. I guess I got distracted saving you, and then I couldn't find the right time."

My hand shakes a little as I take the envelope. All my psychic senses are buzzing with new and exciting sensations. "Thanks. Any time's the right time." My face reddens. I take the envelope and start to slide my finger under the flap.

Erick softly, but desperately, grips my hand. "Maybe wait till you get home?" His big blue eyes plead with me.

"Oh, sure. Yeah. I can totally wait." I nod and try to crutch off the stage without breaking my other leg. "All right, Erick. Thanks for the da—bingo. You're a good caller." I wobble a little on the last step and have to hop like a hokey-pokey reject to regain my balance.

I wave a crutch at Twiggy and make a hasty retreat, replaying my last lame words over and over as I tripod to the Jeep. *You're a good caller.* I'm such a dork!

Back at the bookshop, I set the alarm and check the doors—twice. I don't even remember locking the doors most nights, when I first came to town, but after a towering inferno, a break-in, and some light kidnapping, I've upped my security game.

Once I'm safely inside the apartment, with Pyewacket snuggled up next to me and Grams floating impatiently beside me, I open the envelope.

Inside is a heart-melting homemade Valentine. The front says, "Happy Valentine's Day." But it's the back that turns my insides to warm jelly.

Dear Mitzy,
You're the most fascinating (and infuriating) woman I've ever met. I'm glad you came to Pin Cherry, and I'm glad you're going to stay. You're going to stay, right? Erick.

Grams and I have a good happy cry, and then I slip that carefully crafted card under my pillow and demand that dreamland send me a special episode of the Erick Harper mini-series!

Sweet dreams, to me.

End of Book 4

A NOTE FROM TRIXIE

Another case solved! I'll keep writing them if you keep reading . . .

The best part of "living" in Pin Cherry Harbor continues to be feedback from my early readers. Thank you to my alpha readers/cheerleaders Angel and Michael. HUGE thanks to my fantastic beta readers who continue to give me extremely useful and honest feedback: Veronica McIntyre, Renee Arthur, and Nadine Peterse-Vrijhof. And big "small town" hugs to the world's best ARC Team – Trixie's Mystery ARC Detectives!

Much appreciation to my steadfast editor Philip Newey! Some author's dread edits, but it is always a pleasure to work with Philip, and I look forward to many more. Any errors are my own, as my outdated version of Word insists on showing me only what it likes and when it feels so moved.

Now I'm writing book six in the Mitzy Moon Mysteries series, and I think I may just live in Pin Cherry Harbor forever. Mitzy, Grams, and Pyewacket got into plenty of trouble in book one, *Fries and Alibis*. But I'd have to say that book three, *Wings and Broken Things*, is when most readers say the series becomes unputdownable.

I hope you'll continue to hang out with us.

Trixie Silvertale (January 2020)

CHARMS AND FIREARMS

Mitzy Moon Mysteries 5

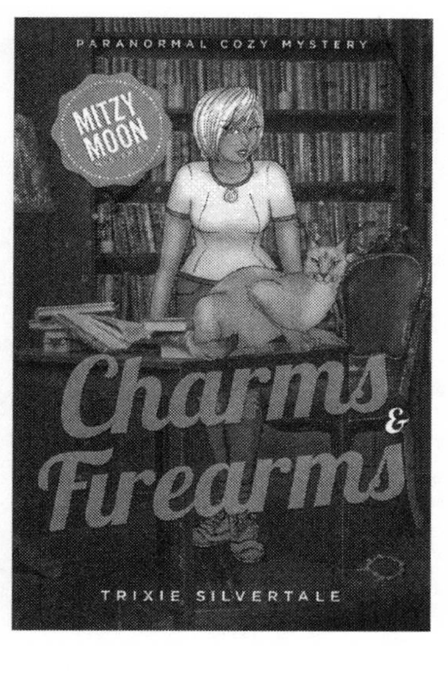

A weekend getaway. A charming present. Will this psychic sleuth find a suitor on the slopes?

Mitzy Moon plans to take a break from snooping and learn to ski. And after receiving a mysterious gift from her travel companion she feels light as a feather. But her heart goes stiff as a board when she faceplants into a corpse.

Racing back to the bookshop to consult her otherworldly helpers, Mitzy is horrified to discover her meddling Ghost-ma is missing. Her spoiled feline seems to ignore her pleas and her alchemist attorney isn't answering either. She can't decide if she's lost her powers or her mind...

Can Mitzy solve a murder without her extrasensory perceptions, or will one misstep put her in the killer's crosshairs?

Charms and Firearms is the fifth book in the hilarious paranormal cozy mystery series, Mitzy Moon Mysteries. If you like snarky heroines, supernatural intrigue, and a dash of romance, then you'll love Trixie Silvertale's twisty whodunits.

Buy *Charms and Firearms* to load a mystery in the chamber today!

Grab yours here!
readerlinks.com/l/962808

SPECIAL INVITATION . . .

Come visit Pin Cherry Harbor!

Get access to the Exclusive Mitzy Moon Mysteries character quiz – free!

Find out which character you are in Pin Cherry Harbor and see if you have what it takes to be part of Mitzy's gang.

This quiz is only available to members of the Paranormal Cozy Club, Trixie Silvertale's reader group.

Click the link below to join the club and get access to the quiz:

Join Trixie's Club
http://trixiesilvertale.com/paranormal-cozy-club/

Once you're in the Club, you'll also be the first to receive updates from Pin Cherry Harbor and access to giveaways, new release announcements, behind-the-scenes secrets, and much more!

THANK YOU!

Trying out a new book is always a risk and I'm thankful that you rolled the dice with Mitzy Moon. If you loved the book, the sweetest thing you can do (*even sweeter than pin cherry pie à la mode*) is to leave a review so that other readers will take a chance on Mitzy and the gang.

Don't feel you have to write a book report. A brief comment like, "Can't wait to read the next book in this series!" will help potential readers make their choice.

Leave a quick review HERE
https://readerlinks.com/l/884697

Thank you kindly, and I'll see you in Pin Cherry Harbor!

ABOUT THE AUTHOR

Trixie Silvertale grew up reading an endless supply of Lilian Jackson Braun, Hardy Boys, and Nancy Drew novels. She loves the amateur sleuths in cozy mysteries and obsesses about all things paranormal. Those two passions unite in her Mitzy Moon Mysteries, and she's thrilled to write them and share them with you.

When she's not consumed by writing, she bakes to fuel her creative engine and pulls weeds in her herb garden to clear her head (*and sometimes she pulls out her hair, but mostly weeds*).

Greetings are welcome:
trixie@trixiesilvertale.com

Made in the USA
Columbia, SC
15 June 2020